REPLACED PARTS

TRANSFORMED NEXUS #1

STEPHANIE HANSEN

To the ICU medical staff who saved my life from streptococcus pneumoniae meningitis.

REPLACED PARTS

ISBN: 978-1-953735-01-0

Fire & Ice Young Adult Books
An Imprint of Melange Books, LLC
White Bear Lake, MN 55110
www.fireandiceya.com

Published in the United States of America.

Cover Design by Caroline Andrus

ACKNOWLEDGMENTS

The transformation this novel has been through would not have been possible without many people. There's no way I can name them all, but I'd like to give it a try. They know how hard I've worked and how many years I've dedicated to books. First, I would like to thank the readers. You breathe life into books and for that I will be ever thankful.

Next, I would like to thank the professionals that helped me trudge through this thing called publishing: everyone at Fire & Ice YA, Carol Cartaino, Dr. Luthi, Michael Neff, Brendan Deneen, Randi Hacker, the Lawrence SCBWI Critique Group, Amy Brewer, Patty Carothers, and Rick Miles.

Next, I would like to thank my friends who saw me through dark times and helped me celebrate the good times too: Cathy Wissing, Sarah Smith, Marianne Guatney, Jeff Sifrit, Steve Martin, and Donna Witters.

Finally, I would like to thank my family for putting up with me: Nate, Ethan, Jenna, Vic Hurlbert, Debra Scarborough, Cassandra Hurlbert, Victor Hurlbert, Vondell Neill, and Peggy Hurlbert. If I inadvertently left someone off the list please let me know so I can add them to the next book.

1
LIBERATION

Sierra

To make a smoke bomb all you need is potassium nitrate, sugar, water and a fuse. Programming holograph messaging to be 'smoke screen projection only' is much more difficult. It's a digital version of invisible ink and completely security cam resistant. I pull up Yesha's incoming call. The smoke allows her image to take shape and it almost feels like she's in the room with me.

"I can't believe you talked me into this, you little gomer."

Yesha frequently begins conversations in the middle, no introduction or formal interrogation into my life. I think that's why I like her.

"It didn't take much to convince you."

"Did you receive the package?"

I hold up the box addressed to me, Sierra, but I've removed the contents.

"Yep, right here, see."

Yesha's laugh is like a chorus of toads with hiccups. Her image vibrates on the smoke.

"That's only the box, you drone bug!"

"I know."

I hold up the syringes that had been inside the box.

"Be careful with those. Check the labels."

I roll a syringe in my hands like Kitchen, one of our home bots, does with pretzel dough.

"One says healing serum, which I asked for. Why does the other say anti?"

"Backup. You always need an emergency abort mission option."

"All right. Thanks!"

Yesha interrupts before I collapse the projection.

"Just be sure not to give the anti if you haven't given the original serum."

After she's gone, I look at my subject.

I shouldn't be doing this, but I find the koala's eyes drawing me in like a poli-magno crash about to happen. It's impossible to turn away.

The Science Olympiad team's going to put me on probation again, which stinks since they're the only local, human friends I have.

Following protocol gets us nowhere, however.

Mom's going to be agitated because this isn't the first time I've broken the rules.

I guide the koala out of the cage, leaving her brothers inside. I have to shake off feelings of jealousy. I don't have any siblings.

"Why ya look so sad?"

Uplifting experiments have given us animals who speak.

"Why do *you* look so sad, Eucarpo?"

The koala glances back at her brothers and then her eyes look up at me past her round, stub nose, and adorable ears.

The sensation of an infant wrapping tiny fingers around mine envelops me. I can't let them endure more unethical testing just so we can have the best DNA combination. I was okay with the testing when the purpose was to help those that were sick and it was beneficial to the koala species, but I can't stomach testing these sweet things just for superficial reasons.

"Hate leaving 'em behind."

"They're going after you if this works."

"What ya mean, if?"

"Healing adaptation experiments have just begun."

"But ya aced the test?"

"Well, yeah, but that was just practice. This is the first time I've used it on a living being. Don't worry, it should all go as planned. I'm just being paranoid."

It would be nice if I could stop blabbering when I'm nervous. Sometimes you just have to go for it and see where the cards fall. That was something my dad used to say. Before he disappeared, he used to tell me lots of things. He's been gone almost a decade, but I might as well as have "Missing Dad" tattooed on my forehead.

"Ya paranoid? Ne'er!"

As she raises the fur above her eyes, I scratch behind her ear, and she leans into it like a bear scratching its back on a tree trunk. Her fur is soft as manufactured silk charmeuse.

"Ah yeah, right dere."

"You sure you're ready for this?"

"It gets us closer to freedom, so I been ready a long time."

She takes another glance at her brothers, and I pick up the syringe with self-healing serum. I begin the sedation process as no one wants to be awake when artery lining fortifies, muscles pull with new agility, and brain tissue encases itself with a biting, thin metal sheet. Another reason I'm jealous of Eucarpo is that she responds to sedation, and I don't.

As Eucarpo drifts into a peaceful sleep, I look out the

school windows and see only the steel and glass of surrounding buildings. Their reflections mirror the sky. Today the unending blue gives the impression of being in the middle of the sea. On gray days, it's as if I've been swallowed by thunderclouds. I can only imagine how green fields would look. People used to love the smell of fresh-cut grass. That was before an asteroid broke through the atmosphere damaging our ecosystem and killing all plants, causing our world to work together to save Earth and its remaining, limited vegetation. The only vegetation left is kept in guarded areas and labs.

I think I can hear the machines used to keep the atmosphere from collapsing but the sound isn't right. Instead of a hum, I hear iron clanging. The serum glides through the syringe into Eucarpo and her breathing intensifies as the cells within her body multiply. No, that isn't the machines. It's locker doors slamming, followed by footsteps of someone coming down the hall. No one should be here now. They should all be at the assembly that I'm skipping. I must finish before anyone else arrives. I look at the oxygen and pulse readings, cringing with every spike. It feels like an hour passes as I look at the screens, but I know it's only been seconds. I count breaths and clock ticks, staring at Eucarpo's oxygen and platelet numbers rising.

"Come on, the science minds keep refreshments in here."

I think I recognize the voice coming down the hall. Every muscle in my body wants to stiffen, but I can't freeze now.

Luckily, the serum is fast acting and Eucarpo's readings are settling. I inject the awakening treatment and then I throw the syringes and all remaining evidence into the incinerator. The burning and sanitizing process will turn these things into energy or something else useful. Eucarpo stirs a little when I hear the door sensor click.

As the voltball captain and visual arts queen walk in, I step in front of Eucarpo.

"Look, we found someone avoiding the assembly," Milcah says as she nudges Danver in the ribs with her elbow.

"Didn't want to surround yourself with the rest of the school body, Sierra?" Danver asks.

"Looks like I'm not the only one."

"Hey, we have authorized passes." Milcah pulls out the sensor card that allowed her access to this room.

Milcah's mom is a World Government politician, consequently she gets whatever she desires, not that she needs much help. She's beautiful in that genetically enhanced kind of way. Nevertheless, it didn't help her when she wanted to sneak into the locker room off hours. I had to override the code for her. It hasn't seemed to put me in her good graces as I'd hoped it would. I roll my eyes.

"I just needed to work on a project. Why are you here?"

"Thought you were banned from working solo," Danver says.

"Like you two don't cross lines now and then. Like cheating on an exam…I still have proof of that you know."

"Yeah, but that seems to be all you do. Is it because your dad ran off? My mom says he escaped with a sexy scientist," Milcah adds.

A bitter taste enters my mouth at the mention of my dad. I pinch the skin on the back of my hand aggressively to keep the haunting premonitions at bay. The media attention the day he vanished causes repeat coverage every anniversary. So, while I'd like to forget, though there's no way I could. Everyone around me is reminded of it too like a reoccurring nightmare.

"Shut up! You don't know anything about him."

"Yeah, I think they're in Barbados studying sea life. Bet you wish you were with him." Danver chuckles, enjoying getting under my skin.

"That's it." I grab a beaker, readying to throw it. Milcah's the smaller target, but Danver's muscles would possibly act as his own shield. Before I can decide whom to throw the beaker at, I hear another voice.

"Who here?" Eucarpo's awake.

As Eucarpo peeks her head around my body, Milcah reaches for her sidearm. Eucarpo jumps to the cage holding her brothers and releases them. They all run for cover. Eucarpo then hops to the table beside Milcah and Danver. Milcah raises her gun. She pulls the trigger, and a tranquilizer shot hits Eucarpo in the abdomen.

"Why did you shoot her?" I ask, outraged, and take a step toward the pair, glad the beaker's still in my hands.

"She was flying at me!"

Eucarpo stirs on the ground and pulls out the tranquilizing dart.

"What have you done?" Danver asks.

"She done what's right," Eucarpo defends me.

"Sound the alarm," Milcah yells.

Her eyes blaze in anger like a mad shooting star.

Danver pulls the alarm lever in the wall. I come to my senses and go to the window next to where Eucarpo's brothers have taken cover.

"Move behind that table."

I usher the koalas away from the window as I set down the beaker to grab a stool. Once they're under the table, I hurl the stool as hard as I can. Glass shatters over me when the window breaks. Eucarpo runs to her brothers.

"Follow me," she says to them as she goes to the window and clears the sill of shards.

I watch her paws break open and bleed. I gently grab one, move the two thumbs aside, and turn it over to apply pressure and stop the bleeding. Before I can grab clotting material, the skin sutures itself.

"Guess the healing adaptation really did work."

"Knew ya could do it."

Eucarpo looks me in the eyes, and I'm gratified with my work's results. She healed fast enough not to experience any pain. The koalas all jump out of the window, finally free.

"What did you do?" Milcah's right next to me watching the koalas jump from ledge to ledge out in the open. She reaches for her sidearm again, but I grab her hand.

"Please don't."

As I see Eucarpo on the street below, I know I've been successful in granting the koalas their wishes. I feel triumphant like when the hypothesized flame test color appears. It's the best emotion and it's the reason I keep breaking the rules. A wrong set right and a pause from the heartbreak.

Principal Skidmore walks in, staring at my hand on Milcah's.

"What's going on here? Why do you have your hand on another student and why's our expensive window smashed to smithereens?"

"I can explain."

"You can explain in detention, young lady."

———

After detention, Mom picks me up from imprisonment and the mood in the car's as thick as drying cement. At a red light, she adjusts the magnets so our poli-magno comes to a halt and drums her fingers on the steering wheel while letting out an exasperated sigh. I open my mouth to speak.

"Just don't," she says before a word escapes past my teeth and I'm sitting there with mouth agape.

"But I," my mouth closes at the sight of her straightforward glare. There must be an academy that teaches mothers this annoying form of communication.

She turns the magnets and we're moving with traffic again, but my heart feels like it stayed where the car stopped. I guess, since Dad left, I've perfected the avoidance of emotions by building a wall that won't crumble, but it can be a lonely existence that way.

"There's always a rationalization as to why you behave the way you do, isn't there."

"It's just, the koalas, if you could've seen what was happening to them with your own eyes."

"Sierra, listen to me closely because you always find an excuse. What are you going to do when they finally kick you out? I've invested too much money sending you to that school."

"I never asked to go to private school."

She grips the steering wheel so tight I'm afraid her handprints will permanently mold into the metal. She doesn't have to answer me because I've heard the response too many times to count. It had been my dad's dream for me to attend private school and then graduate from a prestigious college. Neither of us speak for the rest of the trip. I fold my arms across my chest and stare out the window, wondering if Eucarpo and her brothers made it outside city limits. I should've planned better so I could have escorted them there. I wasn't even able to give her brothers the healing serum. I know Eucarpo, though, and have no doubt she'll protect them at any sign of danger.

Building after building goes by and I'm amazed with this month's artistry. To make up for the lack of vegetation (not confined to labs and other protected areas) the government decided to put abstract art on our buildings. The current piece is of a fire that flows from one building to the next for an entire block. Red turns to blue as we progress. The next block has a peacock with the most colorful feathers. The external wall cells have been adapted to automatically change with the weather and seasons. New artists are chosen each year so that there's a continual sense of surprise and awe.

Mom parks the car in front of our complex and we get out.

I hope she'll break the string of silent reprimand, but I only hear the solar disks rise around the car for charging. As I follow her inside, fearing the punishment she has in store, the quietness continues. Once we're inside, she sets down her briefcase and looks at me. Then she looks at the refrigerator.

"Kitchen, make Brussel sprouts, the cure for stubbornness."

"As you wish, Dr. Perierat."

"Mom, you know there's no actual scientific proof of that, right?"

"You can have a meal to your liking when you stop breaking rules."

Kitchen looks like melted steel that's cooled except with the fluidity of a slithering snake. As Kitchen's metal arms assemble dinner, Mom and I move to the living room.

"Mom, why can't you see that I did the right thing?"

She puts her hand on my shoulder, which I find has tensed. Actually, every muscle in my body is stiff but I hadn't realized it before.

"Ms. Skidmore told me that you said Milcah and Danver insulted your Dad."

I look away, wishing I could fall into myself and become a black hole. I don't want her to see my face because it's full of hate, an emotion she doesn't approve.

"You have to stop sticking up for him. I swear it's as if you think by misbehaving, you'll bring him back."

I look at her, knowing she sees hope like stopping an invasive species, pretty much impossible but not completely unattainable.

"He's not coming back, sweetie. It's been years."

"Don't say that because you can't know it. You don't even know where he is or what happened to him."

She looks down and shakes her head from shoulder to shoulder, a canyon of emotion with everlasting echoes.

"Why don't you go meditate in your room?"

I open my mouth to speak but close it again. She pats my shoulder, walks to her room and logs into her work account from the holograph. Mom probably had to leave work early as a consequence of my behavior. Usually, I take the public transit gliding pod home and she's able to work as late as she needs. I guess I deserve meditation even though I don't get it, but Mom swears by the practice. Her psychological studies have proven it increases mindfulness and builds otherwise dormant cognitive capabilities.

I go to my room and sit on the floor. I bend my legs into the butterfly sitting position, straighten my back and close my eyes. I breathe in, feeling my lungs stretch as far as they can. I breathe out until my chest is compressed, imagining a large, dark circle. Within it forms a violet circle and inside that a blue one. I inhale and exhale again before green, red and yellow circles form. There they freeze and oxygen exchanges without thinking. Finally, the last circle expands like the sun expanding toward the Earth.

I continue as usual but a violent image uploads into my meditation practice. Mom claims that with enough practice I might one day be able to see full pictures, but I never thought I'd master clairvoyance. The image is of Mom running through our house, tears streaming down her face. My eyes pop open as if someone's choking me, and every cell in my body screams to run from my room but I don't want to startle Mom. It could have been a random image and doesn't mean anything at all. I sense it's real, however, and a sudden urgency swarms through me.

When I get to the living room, Mom's on the couch crying but not running.

"Mom, I'm sorry, sincerely, from the bottom of my heart."

"No, your statement was merited, I don't know where he is."

"I know, but I shouldn't have said that."

Now I'm laying my hand on her shoulder, a reversal of roles.

"Are you all right?"

She looks up at me and the sense of urgency resurfaces.

"I just can't live like this. We can't keep hoping that someday he'll be back."

Before I can say a thing, she gets up and walks rapidly across the room. She grabs the multidimensional prism photo hanging on the wall, the last picture taken of all three of us. She looks effervescent in the picture and she hasn't looked nearly as happy since.

"We really should have a more recent photo of you and I up here. Don't you think?"

"Mom?"

She walks to the hallway and removes the first photo. That one is of dad and his Nobel Prize award. I've never imagined that photo not being in its rightful place. His smile in that picture reaches out to you as if the dimples on his cheeks are lunar craters that watch over you while you sleep. She piles photo after photo and marches to the incinerator in the kitchen. They won't fit but she's on a mission.

"I'm taking these to the complex dump. It's time for us to move on."

She's determined. I haven't seen this much zip in her step ever. I never thought she'd succumb to getting rid of his memories. My body shakes like a microscope slide tray when the stage clips are loose, and the focus needs to be shifted. I want to run after her and rip the multidimensional prism photos from her arms. Then I remember she forgot one, so I go to her room knowing I'll find the photo of Dad in her dresser. I open the door, glad she's turned off the World Government sensor. She doesn't believe the government needs an inventory of her clothes. Guess I'm not the only one who breaks the rules.

When I open the drawer, I see the multidimensional prism photo I expected. I pick it up and clasp it to my chest, wanting to fall to the ground and somehow mold it to me. I look again at his questioning eyes. When my dad looks at things, he doesn't see what others do. He's looking for the reason why something is the way it, well, is. The rest of us see gas, liquid and solid matter. He'll look for Jahn-Teller metal, a state most of us outside superconductors don't even think about.

But an angry pain finds its way to my heart. Dad might have run away. He might have meant to leave us. Everything they've claimed about him could be true. Mom's right, we need to move on. I crumple the photo in my fist and the tension releases from my shoulders. It's like he's been a weight I've carried too long. I turn to close the drawer feeling as if I were closing the door to a chapter of my life, but something catches my eye.

Fluttering like a holographic prism shadow, I notice I've disturbed an archaic piece of paper by moving the multidimensional prism photo. When I grab and lift it, I see writing I'd recognize anywhere even though no one really writes now. Dad enjoyed taking notes on the holograph screen with his finger and the slant is the same. I can almost visualize the pen in his hand. Holding this note is like walking into a pyramid tomb, lifting the lid of a sarcophagus and witnessing a mummy rise. It's like I just popped half a dozen endorphin candies in my mouth. Why did Mom keep this from me? For a moment, my happiness is stabbed with pain. How long has she known and what else has she hidden from me? She and I will need to discuss this later but for now I'm thrilled with my discovery.

All my childlike happiness returns as if with this I'm ensured to solve the mystery despite my knowing how futile it might be. I gasp as much in fear as excitement until I realize I can't read what he wrote. It makes no sense until I stare at it longer. Too bad Dad didn't put periods between the individual numbers because it makes deciphering his message much more difficult, but I figure it out. Separate the vowels and consonants, then pair them with prime and composite numbers. It's an old number game we used to play with our naming scheme too.

My dearest Marie,

Cromwell has taken me to Planet Vortex for scientific study that is illegal on Planet Earth. There's no way for me to return. The government allows him to rule here freely and he has taken drastic measures to meet his goal. I will be fine. He needs me. Please take care of yourself and our sweet daughter. I promise to find our baby son. You must try to remain out of the media and continue the front that I have run off. I know this is hard, but you are being watched. I will always love you with all my heart.

Forever yours,
Septimus

Son? What son? I have a brother! How come no one told me? This is more information than I've had about my dad in years. He's alive! He didn't run off with a sexy scientist or at least Cromwell doesn't sound too sexy. I can find him. No, I will find him, and I will ask him about my brother because there's no way Mom's going to crack and tell me, not after she's hidden it from me for this long.

2
STRATEGIZE

Sierra

ONE WEEK LATER AND I'M BACK TO SNEAKING INTO
Mom's room, well not really sneaking because she's at work.
Dad's electronic identification cards drape from tie rack posts
in her closet like vines off a building. I need to scan the cards
and replace them with my picture and a new name. Luckily,
since he was taken against his will, I believe they have him
under false identification. (Or, if he wanted to hide with a love
interest, he'd falsify his identification too.) I shake my head as
if to make the negative thoughts fall away. Either way if he
travelled under his real name, this is going to be much more
difficult. I hold my breath as I hack into the space travel itin-
eraries from the time he was kidnapped (or left and the letter's
just a cover...uh). I'm able to breathe again when I don't find
his name. It almost tears my heart out to replace my dad's
multidimensional prism photo with mine on the screen;
another picture destroyed. In order to make new cards, the

printer will have to shred the old ones. A 3-D printer only works if it has the correct cells to formulate the desired object.

Placing my thumb on the scanner and watching my engineered software replace his print makes it feel like my thumb's touching his. I was able to choose a name easily because my first-grade teacher, Ms. Bucholz, always mistakenly called me Vienna. Vienna Bucholz. If Dad's able to hear the names of arrivals on Planet Vortex, he'll know it's me. The thought of being near him again gives the semblance of an open book, pages fluttering in the wind. Focusing on the details helps. Title: lab specialist, they can begin working at the age of nineteen so I'm only lying by three years. Date of birth: July 20th, 2144. My mom's birthday is July 20th, another flag.

I hack into the social security facial and print recognition system to replace the information within the card's microchip. The 3-D printer spits out two security cards, my dad's originals are now shredded and formed into mine. These flimsy little plastic rectangles are the key to getting Dad (or just go on one stunning trip) and maybe find out about my brother. Now, to get help with the application.

It's so much easier communicating with Yesha from home. I know Mom's turned off the security cams in our bedrooms because, well, that's complete invasion of privacy. So here, in my room, all I have to do is delete history on the computer to make our messages like disappearing ink, which is good because I don't think Mom would appreciate the smell of smoke bomb in the house.

"You can't just apply to be a lab specialist. They're primarily adults, you know."

She worries too much.

"Teach me to be mature like you, oh wise one." Yesha's almost 18 so she's like an adult.

Her face turns resolute.

"Seriously, this is legit."

"I got it."

"Do you really? No wobbles now."

She silently stares me down. "Yeah, okay, yeah."

"Good. So what name are you going to take?"

Yesha helps me fill out the application for the Planet Vortex Medical Research Facility. Anticipation begins to set in like when you're close to proving a theory. I don't want to get too upbeat. I only thought of it because Dad had to have used the recruitment center on the Earth orbit space station to get his letter here. Or, he is just in Barbados (why do these thoughts keep assaulting me?) The odds of my application being accepted are very low. Many doctors apply to the prestigious facility that pays better than almost anywhere else does. I can't keep my eagerness at bay. It helps that Yesha is old enough to apply without falsifying records. She can run through a test application for herself before we finalize mine.

"Bloody hell, it won't let me abort the application."

"What?"

"Look."

She rotates her wrist and the drone bug cam looks at her screen. Sure enough, a pop-up says: *We're sorry for the inconvenience. To decrease the ability to cheat on the aptitude test, all applications require completion.*

"Guess you're going to Vortex with me."

"Bullocks, that was practice. I'm going to ensure your score eclipses mine. My application will be thrown in the incinerator in a flash."

"Ah, come on. It would be nice. We could finally meet in person."

"Someday. But not there."

"Okay, I got it. What's your deal with the place, anyway?"

"Nothing, it's just…"

"Hey, who's that?" Once the screen moved from the test, it showed video feed of Vortex!

"Oh, it's this new thing they're doing at all facilities. It's old though because of the delay of having to go through the station. There's no live communication. This was recorded a while ago."

"He's cute!" I've never found local guys attractive, not that they'd even notice me. This guy is different, so different. He was walking down a hallway in the direction of the camera. He carried a confidence I could never pull off. He was in a lab coat like everyone else around him and yet he stood out. Like he had a trick up his sleeve that no one else knew about except me. For one split moment he looked directly in the camera's direction.

"Hello, Earth to Sierra! Focus much?"

"Oh, sorry. Do you see my dad?"

Yesha tries zooming in for me but the camera won't adjust or move. The purpose of the cameras is to improve transparency into studies but that's not going to work if it only shows 1% of the place. Cog, that would have been nice.

———

As I research Planet Vortex, I remember when I found Dad's hidden note a few weeks ago. My heart rate doubled when I was able to decipher the secret code explaining his location. My mom must've been unable to read the code when she'd received the letter years ago. I'm disappointed she didn't recognize that this paper note, rather than electronic message, indicated that Dad was outside normal bandwidth communication. Now she's even broken her vow to keep his memory alive. I can't believe she took down the multidimensional prism photos of him that we had around the house. The photo I captured and uncrumpled is hidden under my pillow, so I can look at my dad and memorize his features down to the last detail. Since the photo purge, we don't speak of him at all.

That's why I must embark on this mission without her knowing. Moreover, she'd never willingly allow me to take this risk, but, if what the letter's code said is true, I have to go now. He shouldn't be there another second. (And if he's only in Barbados, I swear I will find him so I can kick his butt.)

The monitor at the bottom right of the screen beeps like a ticking bomb. Mom's five minutes away. As I delete the history of Planet Vortex research, I prepare dinner.

"Kitchen, make vegan meatloaf and jacket potatoes, Mom's recipe."

In a British accent, Kitchen replies, "Sierra, the ingredients for this meal are available in the freezer and pantry. Another vegetable should be added to the meatloaf and potatoes for an extra healthy meal."

I stick my tongue out at the computer, who's indubitably right. "What vegetable do you suggest, Kitchen?"

"Asparagus is available in the manufactured, roof garden. It's full of a good few nutrients. Antioxidants prove beneficial for your health."

"Sounds great, please add asparagus." At least Mom will be thrilled.

The computer-generated voice for Kitchen reminds me of the adorable nanny my OLD best friend, Harper, was blessed with as a child. She stayed in the kitchen most of the day yelling snack requests through the halls when I was over. She couldn't do that when I wasn't, because Harper's deaf. Kitchen hangs from the ceiling and isn't able to exit due to the engineering of the apartment. Her metal arms are long enough to reach the lowest pot in the cupboard, but she can fold up into a slot in the wall where no one can see her. I can hear Kitchen's robotic arms moving before I respond. A grocery list pops up on the screen to communicate with the store electronically so items may be replenished via systematic delivery by solar-powered drones.

Light illuminates and sounds float from down the hall, familiar happenings in the only home I've ever known. They pass the big shelf full of scientific collections, including the silver sphere I used to spend hours with as a child. Its lid opens, with a spin at the touch of a light button, revealing clear cylinders that hold stem cells. The digital microscope I used to study everything from dust particles to food shavings sits on the shelf above the sphere. Sometimes I actually find myself yearning the unknown wild while surrounded by these recycled, hard walls. They're home, but something's missing.

Kitchen, in fact, has been somewhat of a parental figure most of my life with my mom working crazy hours and my dad being gone. Milcah and Danver's comments about my dad still burn beneath my skin like a bad bout of shingles. If only I could broadcast his letter (if it's true) so that everyone would know he's not a liar or a cheat but was taken against his will. Unfortunately, there's only one other person among the students who would be able to make out the code, Harper. Reading the letter without understanding the code, one would find his message vague and full of guilt. The gossip would just heighten. I couldn't decode this for them either because it could draw attention to my plans. I would be caught before I ever stepped out the door and Dad's face would forever be missing from our family multidimensional prism photos.

Three minutes and Mom will be here. I run to her closet to retrieve a couple of Dad's medical coats, gripping them with the gentlest touch I'm able to manage.

I take the coats to my closet and hide them within the white section, looking over my shoulder unnecessarily.

"Please add new couvrir to the inventory list." Closet's voice sporadically lapses into French, which is fitting given the country's centuries of fashion expertise. She has the same arms as Kitchen, just placed differently.

"Allow human override and delete history."

"Are you sure, Sierra? Maintaining a log of one's wardrobe is important so that the best possible outfit may be produced."

"Yes, I'm sure."

One minute before she comes through the door, the smell of meatloaf drifts down the hallway as I walk to the kitchen. Mom enters and sets her briefcase on the desk chair as if unloading years of burden. Her beauty contrasts with the dark disks below her eyes. Her strong shoulders are sturdy as the metal buildings of our city.

"Please tell me you've finished your meditation."

"What's one day off?"

She rolls her eyes and lets out a sigh.

"On the way home, the poli-magno had a few glitches. Could you tune it up in the morning or is that too much to ask?"

We both sit down at the table, and her face slackens in a look of surrender. Then Vex rolls up and sets a plate of dinner in front of each of us. The little clopil always has the perfect timing. I see a smile tug at the corner of Mom's mouth; a smirk surfaces from the six feet of dirt. At least I get to enjoy her favorite meal with her before I run off. She lifts her fork but pauses before plunging into the completely satisfying meatloaf.

"So what held you up from meditation this time?"

"Oh nothing, just the Science Olympiad team has the oxygen pill competition thing coming up. I don't know how well we'll do since our pill hasn't been studied abroad."

"Honey, you know we don't have the funds for an Off-Earth trip. You've done marvelously in scientific studies. I'm sure you'll do fine."

"How was your day? Anything you want to talk about?" Perhaps you want to discuss your baby boy that you've never told me about?

"Today was pretty stressful. I'm glad to be home."

She worries about money since my dad's disappearance. She makes enough to provide for us, but their dream of me studying at a prestigious college burdens her. At least I'll be able to remove that with my venture, but she'll be heartbroken. Committing identity theft to go to my dad will render my years of scientific studies useless, if I'm caught. No company will hire a scientist with a felony on their record, no matter how hardworking they may be. The once mouthwatering meatloaf now looks like plastic play food on my plate. I shovel it down anyway to escape further questioning from Mom. We traipse our way through the meal like mice in the desert avoiding vulture detection. There's just one more piece I need to float through the dusty murk.

"Mom, do you mind if I stay with Harper tomorrow? We need to pin down a few details before the competition."

I look to the left to show I'm not lying, which I undoubt-edly am. Mom's studies show that people look to the right when they lie. I twirl my fork on the table, trying to appear anxious, which is in fact what I feel, but I hope she sees it as related to scientific study instead of Dad retrieval. I also want to appear as though I'm not purposefully hiding something from her.

"You're hanging out with Harper again? She always keeps you out of trouble. Of course you can stay with her, but please take some time to relax before finals."

Now I'm able to finish the meal without plastic visuals taking over. She absolutely bought the cover story. She finishes her meal at a record pace too; bet she skipped lunch again. She really works too hard. As we finish our dinner and head to our separate quarters, I want to run up and hug her, but if I do that before bedtime, she'll know something's amiss. Instead, I watch her depart, trying to memorize her tendencies before they're light years away from me. She twirls a lock of her rich, dark brown hair; a habit from her youth she's never let go.

Something that wasn't passed down to me. I'm such a copy of my dad; I wonder how she stands looking at me at all. I do seem to grasp her read on people, the psychology reading did pass down. Even though I'll be away from her, there'll always be that part of her with me.

I head back to the closet and boot-up the Brother 3000 sewing machine. Mom wanted to get rid of it when we acquired our 3-D printer, but I begged to keep the machine. Something about its process gives me peace much like when I'm concentrating on an experiment. After measuring my dad's lab coats, I enter the numbers into the computer. Then I enter my own measurements. Brother extends the cutting board from the wall and projects the coordinates where I should put the coat. Brother's arms and laser cutter move in a choreographed rhythm. The needle of the sewing machine whirs at a speed too fast to follow. I can't believe people once used to do this by hand! Upon completion, Closet chimes in.

"Would you like to try on the coat?"

"Yes, please."

Closet's metal arms pick up the coat and fit it on me. My dad was the last person to wear this, I think as the fine twill fabric brushes against my skin. As I put my right arm in, I sense being closer to him already. Once the coat's on, I look in the digital mirror seeing things as others will. This is the picture my parents have hoped to see since I was born. A ball of guilt wads up in my chest. My muscles tense. About time someone rescued him (or set him straight). It's been almost a decade since I've seen him. No one else has been able to find him, so it's up to me. I don't know which would be worse: never finding him or finding him and not being able to save him. Either way, I must try. I need answers. With one deep breath in, I take the second coat, place it on the cutting board within the same coordinates and hit repeat.

I'm pretty much ready to go. Falling asleep knowing I might see him tomorrow seems impossible.

I imagine what it will be like on Planet Vortex. That desert planet is different from the deserts here on Earth. While it has fractionally less gravity, its clouds are closer to the surface. One would think this would cool the planet, but instead the temperatures are warmer. The multiple moons pull up the lower amount of groundwater, causing a tide like effect of the droplets beneath the surface. The lower clouds and heat cause a humid circulation, making the sand more like what one would find next to a body of water.

"Sierra, are you ready for bed?"

Mom's walking down the hallway to my room. I return the coats and cards to the white section and exit Closet as quickly as I can to throw on pajamas. "Just about."

"Okay, let's say our goodnights now. My eyelids keep drooping so I'm not going to last long, dear."

Now she's at the doorway of my room, and I go and hug her. I don't want to let go. We've made it this long, just the two of us. She hugs with strength and warmth despite her small-ness. I got my height from Dad. When she releases me, I want to pull her back into the hug, but contain myself.

"Goodnight, baby. I love you!"

"I love you too, Mom."

She pauses before departing like she's about to say some-thing. Perhaps she read into my peculiar behavior. Or, she knows I have defiance going on in my head. Then the game's over before it's even begun. I should've planned better for her read on me, but there wasn't enough time. The flights to Vortex only take off monthly (until recently they only took off annually), and the next one's tomorrow. While I found his letter weeks ago, it was only yesterday that I received confirma-tion of my acceptance. If I were forced to sit around and wait another month to perfect my strategy, I'd go insane. There's no way I could hide this from her for another month. She picks a piece of lint off her nightwear and then moves on to go to bed. That was close, unquestionably close.

I delete history again and then brush my teeth; I'm not sure how long it'll be before the next time I use this tooth-brush or brush my hair in front of this mirror, after tomorrow morning. When I lie down, I toss and turn, but must fall asleep quickly because I find myself in a dream.

The Mojave Desert, a favorite vacation spot for my dad that we visited every year before he was gone, spreads out before me. I can taste the dusty grit in my mouth. Moonlike, crater-filled hills with open sandy expanses between them—the smell of wild permeates my being. My dad's eyebrows scrunched in concentration over the Igneous and Metamor-phic erosion. As I hide behind a creosote bush and peek around, I see a Kit Fox lying on the ground. It isn't moving, maybe napping, so I go closer. As I approach, the fox still doesn't move. Then I notice one of its legs is missing and the fur on its back is gone, replaced by burned skin. I think I know why the fox isn't moving but I kneel next to it and check for a pulse anyway. I almost retch right there in the bush. The fox will not be jumping up or trotting around ever again. I'm awakened by a shuddering vulture hiss that repeats over and over.

I roll to my side and say, "snooze."

Then I bolt upright in bed—today's the day.

I throw on the most adult outfit I can muster, and hope Mom doesn't notice I'm wearing the slacks I previously stole from her closet instead of jeans. The Science Olympiad letter jacket should cover up most of my clothes. I delicately roll the coats and cards, attempting to avoid wrinkles, into my back-pack. I also stuff in a large purse I took from Mom's closet. Then I head down to check out the poli-magno, like Mom asked me to.

As I adjust the rotator magnets on our Alembic Momentum 4 with sweat dripping from my forehead, I spot fellow students passing by on the sidewalk next to the polar street. They don't even notice me, not that I look any different than when I'm in our high school testing oxygen pills for the Science Olympiad, but because I'm plain. I'm not one of the kids that stand out or join the student council each year. I'm an extinct species in the social bodies. Not a one of them will notice when I disappear. Within three hours, I should be aboard the SpaceZ Tarragon Shuttle, and none of them will spare a breath asking about my absence. I'm more perplexed by how my mom will survive without me. Maybe Vex will adjust her magnet bearings in my absence. Possibly Kitchen will fix the microchip when the holographs fail. It's been hard enough for us without my dad.

Then, I spot Harper approaching. I roll out from beneath the poli-magno so I'm able to sign and greet her. The first time I met Harper was in kindergarten. An older bully had pushed another kindergartener to the ground and without hesitation Harper helped the kid up. I instantly wanted to be her best friend, but I couldn't talk to her. My dad's the first one who took sign lessons so he could teach me, but Mom didn't like that we could communicate in a way she didn't understand so she quickly learned too.

Hey! How's the photosynthesis study going? I sign.

She turns away, then turns back, pointing to her chest. She mouths, "me?"

I shake my head "yes."

Long time no see, Sierra! Actually, we discovered that more Vitamin D had to be added to the pill for it to work completely.

As she's signing, I drop my phone into her backpack, grateful for her nutty professor tendencies. Harper is brilliant, but completely at a loss when it comes to street smarts. Her backpack is often only half zipped, she's always losing things, and she can't find her Intuos pen even when it's behind her ear. I've been a crappy friend to her lately and this isn't helping. That same ball of guilt begins wadding up, but I imagine the multidimensional prism photo of my dad on his security cards, and it fades away.

Hey, can you cover for me? I told my mom we'd be working on the Science Olympiad project tonight.

What? So, that's why you're talking to me.

I'm sorry, Harper. I've been awful lately. I promise I'll change. Please?

Uh sure, so what are you working on? she asks and then nervously chews her nails.

I can't really get into it now but promise a full report as soon as it's finished. We can hang out a lot more as soon as I'm done.

I'm the worst person on this planet, no, in the universe.

Is that wise? Remember the Koalas? Want detention again?

Yeah, yeah! Everything's going to be all right.

Whatever. I need to get to school.

Thanks. See you!

As she walks off, shaking her head, oblivious to the location sensor I just planted in her backpack, I'm able to breathe. I know she'll be mad that I kept her in the dark about my plans, but I can't put her in danger. She's like the little sister I never had, annoying maybe but a sweetheart, nonetheless. Now if everything else can go this smoothly.

Mom walks out, briefcase in hand. That was close.

"How's it look?"

"The bearings needed adjustment. The magnets should turn without a hitch now. I just need to replace a few things and then you'll be ready. Mom, next time stop at a garage. I don't want you to be stuck in traffic or unable to brake because you're waiting for me."

"You're entirely capable of handling these things and it saves us money."

I'm glad to be under the poli-magno now. If she could see my face, she'd know my comment was meant more as advice she'll need to follow while I'm on another planet. I roll out as soon as I compose myself.

"All done. Have a good day at work."

"You too, sweetie. You should probably get going so you're not late."

"I will, just want to run in and wash up first."

I watch her pull away as I head inside. Part of me wants to run after her and tell her everything, but she wouldn't understand. After washing, I realize I need to leave her a note. I don't want it in the computer so I'm forced to look for a piece of paper and something to write with—both are rarities. I go to her dresser, where I found Dad's note. Sure enough, some paper and an ink pen are just a little further down. I see a few responses she'd attempted to write him peering up at me like lost treasure at the bottom of the sea. So, she had known it was him, even though she couldn't decipher the message.

I don't have enough time to read these or put together a respectable note to Mom. I tell her what I'm doing but omit the location and details. I make it clear how imperative it is that she not call the authorities. Doing so could disrupt my mission and put Dad at risk (or get him busted for falsifying his disappearance). I try to write something meaningful as this may be a piece of me she holds onto for a while but can't seem to find the words.

A term at the facility lasts four Vortex years, though many decide to take up a full-time position there after their term. Communication with other planets is almost impossible because of the limited bandwidth, Counter Friction strings haven't been applied to the planet. I don't plan to stay the entire term, but I'm not sure how long it will take to get Dad. I simply write that I love her and how much I can't wait to have us all back together again. I place the note on my pillow and walk out the door feeling like a voltball player running through the tunnel, adrenaline causing the veins on the side of my forehead to pulse.

As I'm walking down the street, all of a sudden there's a stream of clicks. I look down and see Vex. He has a clear top above his circular, metal trunk. He even has a drone bug that can fly to any household appliance emitting a distress signal. The bug will diagnose the problem so Vex knows what tools to initiate from within his carriage. It's amazing the number of items he holds. He's always providing whatever I need with a sarcastic reply that brings the point home.

"Vex, what are you doing?"

"Sierra, it's preposterous for you to make this journey alone. You need a chaperone. I am fully updated and able to serve you."

"No, Vex, you have to go back and take care of Mom. Delete all history of this journey as soon as you're inside."

"That's not protocol."

"As the only owner present right now, I'm overriding."

"Point noted. Please be careful. There are many dangers on your path."

"I will be. Bye, Vex."

3
VOYAGE

Vienna

My excitement fades like food dye in vinegar during the long public transit gliding pod ride to the Phoenix Station. In my head, I review every fact entered on the Planet Vortex lab specialist application. Vienna Bucholz graduated summa cum laude from Arizona State University where she specialized in medical laboratory studies. She graduated high school and college early. At the age of nineteen, she's decided to begin her career in the medical facility. When the application I sent to a Vortex recruitment center located on an Earth orbit space station was accepted, I was floored. There's no way I could have pulled it off without Yesha's help.

I exit at the third public transit gliding pod station to change. As I speed walk to the public restroom, I take a last look at my home city. The magnetic cars float by without the exhaust fumes or coal burning power of their predecessors. The streets have a simple magnetic paint above the asphalt so that polar projection in tandem with solar energy moves cars instead of fuel or electricity. The buildings that once had been cement are all recycled metal now and tower over me wider at the top than the bottom. The cities' strong buildings on this new Earth poignantly reach for the sky like magnetic sand tiers. Sometimes I imagine my electrons being pulled by the metal. Perhaps one health hazard replaces another with every innovation.

Advertisements suspend in the air above the street by lower weight and therefore higher polarization. I squint my eyes up anxiously. If what I see on the signs hasn't changed, there's no way this will work. It would be like if I had given Eucarpo the anti-self-healing serum without the original first—devastating. If the screens still say what they would to the old me, alarms will go off making it clear that I'm not at school as scheduled. If that happened, I'd be caught for sure. There'd be no way I'd get to Dad.

"The new calorie limitation pill will cause extra calories to pass through the body without adding fatty tissue or aging processes. Those who have found ways around caloric rations will still be able to benefit the medical advancements," the advertisement spouts. It's laboratory specialist targeting media!

Their facial recognition used to feed Science Olympiad and Auto commercials to the screen whenever I passed. A sigh of relief hits me as I realize my hacking into the social security facial/print recognition system and identity change was successful. I'm able to breathe. I notice my hands shaking and massage them to get them to stop. I want to be somewhere private if only for a second.

Once in a restroom, I remove my jacket, put on the lab coat and security card, and insert the remaining coat and card into the purse. I also have one of the Science Olympiad oxygen pills in the purse. Guess they'll receive study abroad. Not that it'll benefit the team much, but I want to know if they work. I inject the jacket and backpack into the incinerator; preparing to hold a silent vigil during the cremation.

"Confirm contents, Vienna Bucholz."

I jump in surprise. A talking incinerator is something I haven't seen before. If it just asked about the contents that must mean a camera is on me. I duck and peek over my shoulder which isn't the smartest move. A camera in the bathroom is crossing the line.

"It's only trash," I hesitantly respond.

"Are there any hazardous materials in your TRASH?"

I think I just detected sarcasm.

"No."

I'm too weirded out to use the mirror in here. I exit and use the window outside instead. I'd rather be among dozens of human strangers than that camera. At least I can look them in the eye. I prop my dark chestnut hair in an organized bun and add non-script glasses. I don't really need them and most people that do have surgery to correct their sight. Still a few people enjoy the feel of glasses or maybe fear surgery. I wear them because they make me appear older. I hop onto the next public transit gliding pod at the same stop.

As we near the final station, I can see a line of people waiting to board the vans that'll take us to the launching sites. Now the excitement bubbles back as if vinegar was dropped into a cup of baking soda. When you watch an experiment like this, you're always afraid the mixture will flow over the beaker, even while knowing the measurements used shouldn't allow this to happen.

———

"Next."

I hand the attendant my security card and press my thumb into the print scanner. He studies both for a brief moment as I hold my breath.

"Vienna Bucholz, Arizona State. Hey, is ol' Dr. Bobek still there? What a hoot that guy was," the attendant said.

I clasp my hands together to hide the shaking. "Must have retired."

"Thought he'd never do that. What hotshot replaced him? Those had to be some big shoes to fill."

I didn't think to research that closely. Out of all the odds, the first person I speak with on this mission graduated from State too. It would have been nice if I could have just snuck onto the cargo hatch, but I know the particle scan upon the ship's reentry to Earth would sound the alarm and begin a being-hunt. I need to respond quickly in order to appear confident in my statement or at least that's what I've learned from Mom.

"Dr. McPike's a new professor, and he's spot on with research."

Well that was stupid. I shouldn't have given the name of my high school teacher. Now he might be able to pinpoint my true identity.

"He'd have to be. Okay, enjoy your flight, Vienna. You're in van C. Only one going to Vortex. Next."

I'm able to slow my breathing as I take a step into the van feeling glad to be on board. By the time that guy looks into my answer, I'll be light years away. He'll have forgotten my comments by then. More than likely he'll be seeing quite a few people by the look of the line that remains. Where are all the other vans headed?

Then I see her. Yesha's halfway back on the right. It's so weird meeting someone you've only known digitally. I wonder if she'll like me. The seat next to her is open. As I approach, she spots me.

"Lookie, the little pipsqueak actually does exist."

"Your highness, in the flesh."

I grandly bow in front of Yesha and she smacks me on the shoulder.

"Can't believe they still hired me. It's ridiculous."

"You going to hate me forever about that?"

She scoots over and pats the seat beside her. "Sit down."

As I sit, she holds onto my forearm. There's a multidimensional prism note between her hand and my coat. I take the note and begin to unfold it. I gasp as I realize what it is: blueprints of the facility. Yesha puts her hand on the note and lowers it out of anyone's view. Then she whispers.

"Not here and be sure to memorize it and then encrypt it the second after."

As we board the SpaceZ Tarragon Shuttle, I feel like a child waiting in line for a binary power coaster. Four metal towers surround the liftoff site, spreading long shadows. The shuttle has a flat, round nose and the smoothness of its body reminds me of a seal. The small wings slant similar to what I imagine a Mom would look like stretching her arms behind her shoulders in order to hug five children at one time. The space elevator is viewable in the distance appearing as if a ladder hinges on the clouds.

"To the right," a man dressed in an aviation jumpsuit says. He points to the shuttle seat I'm to take. He has a stethoscope around his neck which I find odd for a flight crew member.

I walk that way but when Yesha follows me, the man holds up his arm to stop her and points to the left.

"You're to sit over there."

I notice his name badge says Quintus. When he turns to the next person in line, Yesha rolls her eyes. Cog, I'd hoped we could sit next to each other.

When we lift off, I have the sensation of a being in a binary power coaster on a steep hill but heading upward rather than down. The antimatter pressure system activation and booster ignition shake the entire shuttle far beyond clearing the towers. Clouds zoom by and I swear every proton moves away from me. I'm saddened that my seat only faces forward. I'm unable to watch my home planet turn into a speck of dust, but I know it's necessary so the G-forces will hit me front to back and be benign. G-forces head to toe or the reverse can be deadly.

The Moon streaks by when fusion propulsion kicks in and we pass at the speed of light while the seat straps dig into my skin. The crew claimed they had to put them at the tightest setting because of my lean stature. If they only knew my stature was due to my being sixteen instead of nineteen, they'd throw me into the space vacuum for sure for falsifying identification records. And I wouldn't get a juvenile hearing as the World Government changed the legal age of adulthood from eighteen to sixteen. I'm amazed my disguise as a scientific lab specialist has worked this far. If Mom knew that I was travelling astronomical units away to save Dad, she'd ground me to Earth for a life sentence. I should be practicing the lines I'll have to regurgitate from my lab studies during the flight, but I can't keep my eyes away from the porthole window.

Mars is a blip that I think I catch. As the rest of the Planets zoom by while we travel at superluminal speed, I'm able to sense leaving the Heliosphere's bright light and passing the Oort Cloud's milky haze. The shuttle uses Fifth Dimension Friction Inhibitors and the warp drive sends a tiny ripple of energy through the cab. It's a beautiful dark outside with streams of light from the stars while we drive through contracting space-time. I wonder what Planet Vortex will be like.

"Hey, your nose is bleeding," the passenger sitting next to me says with a lisp while pointing at my nose. She grabs a tissue from the console in her seat and hands it to me.

I lift my hand to my upper lip in time to catch the warm liquid, then use the tissue to clean up the mess. I hold it there for a while until I think it's safe to remove. "Did I get it all?"

"Mostly, there's just one more spot right below your nose." She points to her own to show me where to wipe. I notice she's wearing a Pi necklace.

"Thank you! What's your name?"

"I'm Pixie. What's yours? Did you apply to be a scientist?"

She has a small chin. She looks a little like Harper except for a wider forehead and bigger, round eyes. I've heard statisticians have formulated a way to breathe through their eyes in order to answer questions faster during Stat Races. I can't help but stare, trying to find the rhythmic up and down flow in her eye muscles, just as you look at a rescued drowning victim, searching for signs of life. For some reason, statisticians seem in need at the Medical Facility on Vortex.

"I'm S…Vienna. I'm to be a lab specialist." I should've practiced saying Vienna aloud. That almost slip was a near giveaway.

"Oh, you're going to be studying medicines, patients and things of that sort. I enjoy theory and statistics more."

"Yeah, I like to see the mechanics. How will you be applying Statistics to the Medical Research?"

"Well, stats can pinpoint the probability of research before money has been spent on studies."

"What else have you studied?"

"Beside the chromosomal defects of clones, I've studied conscience and sub-conscience survival after death."

"That had to be interesting. What did you see at the molecular level?"

She doesn't answer me but stares out the port window as the shuttle slows.

"Oh look, there's Vortex."

Sometimes a new place seems oddly familiar the first time you see it. I don't get that sense with Vortex. It's strange to see more than one moon in the daylight of all times. But, residents of this sepia planet are quite accustomed to it.

As we enter the atmosphere making route to land, the mosaic of shadows from the moons is a bit of a challenge for my eyes, but I manage to spot a couple of succulents. They're few and far between but ten times the size of the ones at home. Their plump leaves are one of the sparse sources of drinking water on Planet Vortex. With them, I have more bases for oxygen refill. The Science Olympiad pill will only last so long (if it works).

As we near the landing site, everyone else falls quickly to sleep. There must be an anesthesia gas entering through the vents. It's the only thing that makes sense. Why else would everyone simultaneously lose consciousness? Then a masked crew begins their rounds. I don't know why, but I decide not to mention to them that I'm unresponsive to such a thing. I pretend to be asleep just as the other passengers to keep up pretenses. That's when I hear the crew discussing different passengers. Looking over bodies to see who'll be the best fit, for what—I'm not sure. They discuss a passenger on the other side of the ship. It's hard to tell who they're talking about with my eyes closed. I listen while I try to keep my eyelids from fluttering. A male voice from the crew is the first to speak. It sounds like that Quintus guy.

"Is he a fit?"

Then a woman responds, "Yeah. He's healthy, smart, and has the right blood type."

"I don't understand why we have to do this."

"Do you have the invisible ink?" Hey, invisible ink's my trick! What are they up to?

"Right here."

"You able to do the tattoo?"

"Yeah, but I still feel like we shouldn't."

"Don't talk so loud. You know we're being watched, even now."

"Whatever."

When I hear the buzz of the tattoo gun, it feels like an assault from internet bullies hiding behind masks. It's like the media after my dad's disappearance, the mocking from the kids at school, and people I don't even know trying to discover my most intimate secrets. All these things rip me apart.

They approach my seat and begin talking again. When I hear tools jostling around, I peek my eyes open. The woman's name badge says Lucretia. I close my eyes completely when Quintus speaks.

"What about her? She's young and healthy."

"No, she's to wait until later," Lucretia responds. "Graduated with high rankings. Dr. Cromwell wants to see what she can do in a lab."

It's so hard to stay still as they discuss me. It's like right before a doctor resets your broken bone; impossible to relax, waiting for the snap. Once they've stepped away I hear the tattoo gun again. Part of me wants to punch them in their faces, take over the shuttle, and head back home. But then, my dad would still be stuck on this planet where apparently they tattoo people without their consent and who knows what else. I try to take an unnoticeable deep breath in, softly and slowly so the expansion of my lungs remains out of sight.

Landing is like I'm tethered to this planet. The lights brighten and my seat adjusts to an upright position. I open my eyelids as small as I can and see those around me moving. I fully open my eyes to look around. I don't see the crew. I try to look around to see if I can see markings of a tattoo, but no one seems to have red, raised skin. They must have used a microscopic laser gun, cog it.

I have to tell someone about what I heard, but everyone seems to have a zoned-out gaze. They're not fully awake yet, which means I shouldn't be either. I focus on the wall in front of me. The hexagonal molding reminds me of a beehive. A voice over the intercom instructs all passengers to swallow a pill engineered for our survival on Planet Vortex. During the announcement, a tray slides out in front of me with a purple capsule. Then a metal beam from the ceiling lowers a glass of water onto the tray.

I pick up the pill and hold it for a few seconds, wondering what ingredients are inside. Why should I trust this pill? What if it'll mutate my body so that it's only acclimated to the environment of this planet? I don't have time; everyone else has taken their pill. If I hesitate a moment longer, they'll know. I swallow the pill with the water, trying not to eye it too long. I'll need hydration, but I struggle to find even the water trustworthy.

Then strange, gray creatures enter the area. They're muscular and armed. At first glance, they appear to be alien cavepeople. As they come closer, I spot hairy moles all over their bodies, the size of the average pinky tip, small hills sprouting vegetation. Their weight-trainer like bodies contrast with their small, mallard-shaped heads. They don't have beaks, but their jaws jut out.

The voice on the intercom states, "Welcome, new arrivals. Your escorts into the medical facility have boarded."

As the restraints lift off my shoulders, I want to massage my muscles. Everyone else just stands up, so I do the same.

One of our escorts says, "Follow us." His voice is gruff, as if his vocal cords have swelled from excessive use.

As we step out onto sand, I'm instantly hit with the

memory of my dad breaking open a geode for me to see. The brightness that shined off the crystals was much like the light now. My eyes slowly adjust from the darkness of the flight. The smell of dirty sand and nature juxtaposes my home in an actually comforting way. Even though we're under an awning stretching over our path all the way to our destination, I feel as though the heat might scorch me. The heat shivers through the red tinted land. When I look back at our aircraft, I don't see signs of population for miles, unless it's hiding behind rock, only desolation. Somewhere, beyond reach is this planet's population. Even on another planet, I still feel like a silo because on Earth I'd been surrounded yet all alone.

The escort commands the group, "Keep up," and as I peer his way, I see a wall. It reminds me of an ancient Arabian city with intricate columns every twenty feet, taller at the corners, but with the gray wall of a moated castle. The awning should extend over a drawbridge. Perhaps there was one before, but it evaporated in this planet's temperatures. It's humid as if the moat could be in the air particles around me. Instead of an open expanse like the Mojave Desert, this land seems to be interrupted with rocky hills as if the hills were buildings of a city.

Then I see a vulture fly by and gasp. Wings with knife-like feathers stretch out in front of my eyes. Its feet look strong enough to carry a military tank. These alien vultures have wingspans longer than the length of a man, and beaks the size of my head. Beaks sharp as a blade forged by the most skilled metal printer, the Blacksmith 1000. Next, an alien camel walks around the corner of the wall. Its legs move elegantly without shaking its humps.

As we enter the Planet Vortex Medical Facility, I notice the multiple fences. The exterior is chain link with curled barbwire on top. The sun bounces off it in a blinding beam. It opens to a wall of sepia cinder block. Guards march between the fences protecting the facility. I notice a couple relieving other guards as if they're working in shifts. All I can picture are prisons on Earth. I feel as though I should be in hand and ankle electric cuffs. Everyone follows the guards like zombies as we walk through the gates, and I attempt to mimic their moves, but can't hold back a gasp when the facility reveals itself. No building in my present day and planet could resemble this green glass and cement castle. The first door opens on its computer-programmed sliders.

When we enter the facility, a man moves his hand to rub the back of his long, sun-reddened neck. I take advantage and rub my shoulders too. I want to relax and settle into this place but can't forget the tattoos. I want to talk to Yesha, but the guards seem to be on a tight schedule. Plus, we're not really supposed to know one another anyway. The guards lead us down a hallway. Many of the rooms we pass have glass windows so we are able to see what's going on in them. There's a watermelon smell but I can't figure out from where it's coming.

The guard with the gruff voice informs us about each room. "This is where cell manipulation happens. You really have to squint your eyes to witness the Femtotechnology." What a horrible attempt at humor. I see people in scrubs focused on their work. I keep looking for a sign of my dad, but see only microscopes, plastic tubes, syringes, and other scientific study equipment. Where could he be?

"We're going to give you a tour of the facility," the guard says. "We'll point out where each of you will be assigned as we go. Then we'll head to the cafeteria for dinner. Your personal effects have already been moved to your individual quarters. After you eat, we'll escort you there. Tomorrow you'll take a class and then begin working."

"What's the class for? We've had years of study. Can't we just dive right into the work?" Yesha asks.

Yesha is tall like me except with dirty blond hair. I'd wanted to talk to her but didn't want to raise any alarm with the guards. Looks like she doesn't care as much about that. Probably because she doesn't know about the tattoos. I should have told her.

The guard walks up to her, setting his hand on a chain whip coiled at his belt. His arm muscles ripple, and I'm caught in a moment of pure terror. Instead of pieces of me freezing, every sense is heightened. I can hear the sand hit the external windows with a gust of wind. As he stands a foot in front of her, he gives her a stone-cold look.

"You will follow orders here. The regimen is set to preserve every study and formulate the best results. What's your name?"

She returns his cold look with one of defiance, "I'm Yesha. I understand the need for strict standards but have years of proper study. Take a look at my records."

I notice she's picking at her cuticles despite her strong response and she holds her shoulders firmly up. Why is she agitating this guy? I hope she's not trying to get kicked out. I know she doesn't like this place, but I need her, especially now.

"Well, Yesha, that may be true, but everyone's to follow these commands or there will be repercussions. Do I make myself clear?"

"Yes," she replies curtly, and we proceed to tour the rest of the facility.

It's killing me not being able to run up and talk to her. We've had more communication digitally than in real life (IRL). All of the passengers are eerily silent for the remainder of the tour. No more questions are asked, as if everyone's afraid of agitating our escort. The escort team uses codes to open the door of each sector. We're informed that security cards will be given to us for our assigned locations. I'm only allowed in certain areas. Uh, this place is difficult! I'm surprised we don't need retina scans to access areas.

As if on cue, one of the facility staff walks up with a bundle of cards. She's round and her cheeks are red in a constant blush. She walks around asking for identity and handing out cards. When she approaches me, she looks deep into my eyes as if she can read my thoughts. I hesitate to grab the card she's handing me. Instead of using a harsh voice like the guard to remind me to take the card, she simply places the lanyard over my head and pats my shoulder.

"There, there, Cherie. Things will feel normal here before you know it," she says and with a warm nod departs.

When the tour ends, and the intimidating guard tells us we're headed to the cafeteria, I recall a few passageways we didn't go down. Their doors had been a deep Brunswick green instead of the chartreuse of the other doors. They also had fingerprint scans unlike the others. I wonder if my dad's behind one of those because I didn't see him during the entire tour. Come to think of it, the entire tour was quite limited. What's going on behind the other doors?

"Here's the cafeteria. Grab a tray and go through the line. Your seats will be with the rest of the residents," the brash guard instructs.

Instead of one sliding door, there are two here; kind of like French doors except instead of flapping open into a beautiful manufactured garden, the electronic suction reveals more of the placid environment where we've spent the last hour. I walk into a large cafeteria; it reminds me of the one from my high school except for the alien desert beyond the windows. Identical long tables with benches are in strategic rows. Except instead of plastic and metal, the tables and benches are wooden almost custom made as if someone here needed an ounce of décor. I wonder how they imported this much. After debating between the fungi-looking meatloaf and the porridge that moves like there are caterpillars inside, I look for a place to sit, gripping my bright orange tray. I try to find Yesha.

Then I see a man like no man I've seen before. His arteries are all outside his skin. I stumble on my own feet at the shock of the sight of him. I almost fall to the ground, but a bionic hand grabs my arm before I collapse. When I lift up my head to see my hero, I look into eyes as green as the northern lights. It's as if I could get lost staring into his eyes and yet feel like I'm safe at home too. They're warmly mysterious, if such a thing is possible. It's *the* guy I spotted during the application process.

"I don't usually issue warnings to be careful while walking, but for you, I'll make an exception," my savior says. "Name's Al."

I smile and blush at his remark. *Stupid.* Why is it that I can pass a Physics test with flying colors and then act like a complete sap in front of a guy? It doesn't seem to faze him. I'm not sure if that's a good thing, though.

"Thank you." I'm about to give my real name when I recall my purpose here. "I'm Vienna."

He takes a seat at the table in front of us, and gestures for me to sit next to him. It's the table with the artery man. Luckily, artery man doesn't look at me as I sit. If he did, he'd catch me trying to see his pulse. No one at the table raises an eye when I sit and try to eat my food but can't.

Al wolfs down his food as though he hasn't eaten in days while I poke at what looks like meatloaf. It barely has any resemblance to the vegan meatloaf Mom and I had last night. I wonder what's actually in it. The thought of my last meal with Mom erases any appetite I might have had. Then a familiar-looking man walks to the center of the room, and everyone becomes still staring in his direction. He's not a big man, but his ability to draw attention is impressive. He has a stiff, militaristic stance that demands respect.

His booming voice fills the area. "Doctors and patients, thank you for fulfilling your duties. We have successfully found the process to end third strain Nipah Virus on Planet Earth today. Our other studies continue to look promising. Keep up the good work."

As he closes, a doctor begins to choke on his food. Someone next to him exercises the Heimlich maneuver, and he's quickly breathing again.

"Something…in…the…meatloaf," he has to gasp between words, still out of breath from choking.

I know his voice. It's Quintus. He's the doctor who questioned processes at the medical facility during the trip on the SpaceZ Tarragon shuttle.

The man with the booming voice looks at a guard and quickly nods his head to the right. Immediately the guard is on Quintus. The guard's gray and muscular arms encase him. As the guard begins to take him away, I notice a woman from his table squish her camel milk carton. It's Lucretia. It's got to be.

When the guard has removed Quintus from the premises, Al shoves his tray away from him. I'm surprised he's capable of doing this after his previous ravenous behavior. Within seconds, every other tray at our table is shoved away. I shove mine away too, though I haven't touched a thing. The man who made the announcement has turned away, and I swear from this table every look at the back of his head is full of daggers. I don't understand why they're upset about guards taking a man for medical attention except the guard did seem a little forceful. And, I remember what Lucretia told Quintus on board the shuttle. "You know we're being watched".

That's when it hits me. Why would a cafeteria full of gifted scientists stay when they hate it so much? Most don't know. The other tables around me have not seemed to react. They're still eating. I look around more and see an armed guard stationed at every exit. Surely attempted extraction would be met with violent disapproval. Had I looked to see if a code or fingerprint was needed to be able to exit this place when we first entered? No. I'm such an idiot. I've just walked right into the spider's web. This is worse than what I had imagined when I read Dad's letter. I must have blocked the truth out, not wanting to see pain inflicted on him. My excitement at the thought of seeing him and possibly returning him home clouded my vision. Here I am pretending to be an adult when I feel more like a child than I ever have before.

4

TIME LOOP

Al

It made me sick watching my parents together as a boy. They finished each other's sentences and seemed to move in step together. While my dad was cooking my mom would hand him ingredients just as he needed them. And he picked up a bottle of paint from the store before she even knew the color was about out. And yet, they were opposites. He liked coal and fire for barbequing, the grease dripping from tongs. She liked the smell of fresh cut peppers and pulled daisies in a vase. I completely had been looking for a break from their sappy puppy love. That is until they were gone.

I may be twenty, but I still remember what it was like the day the World Government took over. I had been hiding in my tree house on Planet Funen while my mom was planting, and my dad was working on our car. Not a hybrid or some poli-magno but a real, genuine, gasoline fed car. Funen is the place of relics. My dad claimed we transported there because it reminded him of life in the good ol' days. He said there had been a time on Earth that was perfect. A time he had never lived but knew about because of the classic tales his grandfather had told. It was a time when people were free of bias, prejudice, and misfit judgement. A time when things were equally fair, and everyone had the same opportunities available to them. But times of such perfection rarely last.

Back then, it had been the collaborative automation software programs that led to the conclusion. Because even in a time of peace, there's always one bad apple. And so, with home, office, and public automation systems through complete and connected innovations, the bad apple had access to everything. A simple synchronization command worm to the hub brought destruction, loss, and death.

Before this, Funen came close to perfection. We worked with technology and science. Stem cells cured diabetes and macular degeneration. It cured most diseases. But, when you have something that powerful, you must protect it otherwise it will turn. When the enforcers pulled my dad out from under the hood of the car, I knew something was wrong. I could sense it in my bones. They marched him over to my mom, her gloved hands covered in the soil she nurtured.

"Where is it?" they yelled at my dad over and over. They held him, and they cuffed him.

When my dad didn't answer the third time an enforcer pulled out a gun. I remember the loud bang. It's what I wake to many mornings. Her body seemed to fall in slow motion delicately into the plants she tended. I could have sworn the stems and leaves bent her direction to return the favor as she had nurtured them all her life. A life that was now horribly and inextricably over.

My dad screamed a scream no one wants to hear. He elbowed an enforcer, knocked the gun out of another's hand, and hit another one in the head with the cuffs. But, he was outnumbered and when he was one second too slow to turn and see an enforcer retrieve a gun, it was a mistake in which he wouldn't recover. And, at that moment, I knew all things wrong were about to hit me in the face but that they'd be unable to bounce away as nothing would be there. This was going to hollow me out. They might as well shoot me too. The second gunshot ringing out woke me from my fear trance.

I waited until the enforcers went into the house to look for whatever they were searching and then hightailed it. I just kept running and running until my legs wouldn't take me any further. I wound up at a school for children without a place to sleep. I can't really complain much. It's what got me here on Planet Vortex. That's how I met Viscerous and Albina.

———

"Al, are you paying attention?" Albina asks me while walking over to me. She has this way about her, elegant and strong like a competitive swimmer racing across the water but without causing any ripples. She's graceful yet sturdy.

"Of course, why?"

She points to the holograph screen. "You've been staring at the same image for five minutes."

"Well, it's an interesting one."

"Right, that's the home screen, you nimrod."

She walks by and ruffles my hair as I get to work. Viscerous and Albina smile at one another as he swipes her screen to more findings after kissing Albina on top of her head.

"Look, Al, this one's showing less resistance."

I come over and look at the complete blood culture, CBC, findings and sure enough, before I can think a second more, he's got his arm around my neck giving me a noogy, rubbing his fist on my head.

"Hey, man, you're messing up my hair." I push him away but can't hold back the smile.

It fades when I look at the results more.

"You think this will put an end to it all?" I ask.

"Yeah, right," Albina scoffs.

"You're thinking down the right line," Viscerous counters.

Albina slaps Viscerous on the arm. He then begins rubbing her shoulders.

"He'll never take these. It has to be 100%. He expects nothing less than flawlessness."

"You say it like it's something to be admired," Albina says with a sneer, nonetheless.

"Yeah, but what if we could get this information out of here," Viscerous begins.

"Impossible," Albina says.

"Not entirely," I say with a smirk.

———

I crawl through the tunnels hoping to find out who will be scheduled on the next flight. If we can get a message through to anywhere outside Planet Vortex, we might have a chance to save lives. It's difficult to crawl quietly in the small, plastic tunnels. The beauty of bionic limbs though is that they can bend any way you like. I get to the vent faster than my normal pace.

"...I've never seen findings like this...they're profound," the Representative tells Dr. Cromwell.

They showed up at the facility more and more lately. A shiver runs through me. Anytime a government official is nearby my mood becomes uneasy, like hair when you're near an electric field.

"Don't touch that," Cromwell says as he removes a tube

from the Representative's hands. "It's far from complete, still room for error."

"You worry too much. This is incredible." Representatives all sound like slimy snakes to me and this one doesn't differ.

"But, it has to be tested further. Altering the evolution of a virus before it's occurred is unprecedented." I have to admit, part of me respects that Cromwell steers a tight ship, especially when it goes against a government official. Nope, he still disgusts me. No matter how successful he may be, he'll always be corrupt in my mind. As my dad said, it's the constant struggle between power and morals. In which my mom countered, what's the point of power if you can't sleep at night.

"Yeah, and the tariffs are gone. We're bleeding money. There's no way we can expand to another planet on current funds. This has to sell." So this is the push for such urgent drive in studies…money, it's always money.

"And what if it blows up in our faces? I just need a couple weeks more. I have the best scientists tasked to this." As much as I dislike Cromwell, I like that he's standing up against this Representative jerk. Now, if they could just take each other out.

———

I continue down the tunnel in order to see if the administration office is scheduling the next flight. I'll never get over the smells of Planet Vortex. Plastic smells like watermelon! My appetite increases the further I crawl. Finally, I arrive at the administration office.

"How's this one?" Cora says. Cora gives off a vibe like she should be everyone's grandmother baking us cookies instead of working for the vile Dr. Cromwell. It's as if she's the fabled Mrs. Claus from old Earth.

"Wow, she fits the bill. Cromwell even made a note to accept this one," another administrator says.

I scoot a little further to see the screen. There's a picture of a woman close to my age. She has long, dark, copper, wavy hair and a button nose. Her lower lip's a little tense like she's deep in concentration. Looks like the facility's cover of great pay is still working. It's hooked in another sap. I almost forget to maneuver myself to see the scheduled staff for the flight.

"Well then, Vienna Bucholz, welcome to Vortex." Cora taps the accept button, highlighting it on the screen.

One more inch. Ah, there it is, the schedule. Times and dates are listed first. Next, the roster for the first flight. I squint my eyes: "Q", "U", "I" but before I can read further Cora grabs the collapsible tablet. It has to be Quintus. Now, all I need to do is get to him before the scheduled flight, in secret.

5
AWAKENING

Vienna

"Newcomers first, line up at the red door," the same tour escort addresses the cafeteria. "Everyone else line up after them."

I look around to find my party. The newcomers are easy to locate, as everyone else appears to be wearing a uniform. I spot Yesha and stand to head in her direction.

"See you around, Vienna," Al says with a grim smile. Without his previous demeanor, his eyes seem to have dimmed like a virtual reality forest at dusk. I find myself missing him.

"What part of the medical facility do you work in?" I ask him, but a guard clears his throat. When I look up at the guard, I'm unable to form any words. Otherwise, I'd tell Al goodbye. The smell of robust artificial pine seems to linger after stepping away from Al. In fact, it doesn't diminish with every step away from him as I expected but lingers and seems to fill my memory space.

Walking toward the red door feels off and not just because it appears like a target surrounded by the gray, smooth walls. All of the other doors have been a greenish color. There seem to be suits and protective gear in racks next to the door.

I whisper to Yesha when I'm close enough. "What do you think of this place?"

"I think the security detail is absolute bonkers, but did you hear what the facility discovered today? I can't wait until I'm in the lab and able to research." She strums her fingers on her thigh as if guitar strings lay within her pants as she responds.

"I thought you didn't want to be here?"

The guard clears his throat again. It's as if he's Medusa, and his stare will turn us into stone. I quickly look at the back in front of me to avoid eye contact. I want to turn around and see Al one more time, but I'm afraid this will just disgruntle the guard more. Instead, I attempt to decipher whether the material in front of me came from a 3-D printer or a sewing machine.

"As stated before, we are going to take you to your individual quarters now. You may have noticed this door's color is different from the others we've seen. That's because it leads to outside the facility. If you haven't taken a pill to prepare your body for this planet's environment within the past twenty-four hours, you don't want to go through a red door. Oh, and do not look up. Got it?"

We all nod in unison as he opens the door, becoming servants. It's dark. I hadn't noticed the sunset while in the cafeteria. I'd been preoccupied, but this I would expect to catch my attention.

"We're in the middle of a solar eclipse. Planet Vortex has six moons, so they're more common than on Earth. It does mean we have the same distance equilibrium as Earth. You're lucky though. It's not often we witness a total solar eclipse. We usually only see partial eclipses."

He finishes as the last of us step outside with a second guard. The second guard is unlike any of the others I've seen thus far. He has more human characteristics. He's a darker gray and it accentuates every facial feature and curve of his body. He looks at me and I quickly turn away. I can't believe he caught me. I was completely gawking. How embarrassing!

It is cool compared to the torrid heat upon arrival here. We're surrounded by the castle like wall, but before the wall are rocky hills with cliffs jutting out into the dark sky. Stunted hills are sprouted everywhere, full of holes like they had played laser tag except not with toys. Every hole has a lit, partial sphere around it, incubators glittering the hills. I find myself mentally calling them incubators because they remind me of the ones that held little chicks in Elementary school. There are also lit rails connecting each incubator to the facility.

The guard pulls up a holograph screen at a podium near the external side of the door. He types something in, and I try to use my height to see what it is. I recognize it as an algorithm. I'm unable to decipher it completely this time, but I should be able to after watching him a couple more times. There may be a glimmer of hope residing in this grim facility.

Next, a cross between a hover bike and a mini railcar glides to a halt on the lit rails in front of us. I didn't think gravity was exceptionally different here. Why do they need rails? Is it just to help keep us captive, or is there some other purpose? I wonder if I'll have free time to test this theory. Shuttles come and go here so there must be an explanation.

The second, breathtaking yet scary guard mounts the car in the front and inserts his identification card below the handlebars. There are two seats behind him. "Yesha and Vienna are to go with me first. We'll have to make a few trips to take all of you to your quarters." His voice is deep and assertive, but not as brash as the other guard.

Yesha gestures for me to board first. Guess she doesn't want to be near the guard. Does she think that I do? I'll give in, this one time. But, I feel further away from Yesha than I did when we only saw each other digitally. I put a foot on a pedal and swing my other around. I'm thankful for the bar between the guard and me. I grab it and wait for Yesha to board. The car takes off, and I'm glad to be holding onto the bar. I hear Yesha yelp and grab her own. Wonder if she's still happy with choosing the rear seat?

As we pass some of the incubators, I try to see inside. They're frosted or something so though I'm able to make out shapes; I can't tell what they are. We come to a stop at one halfway up the hill. There's another screen and this time I'm close enough to see the cryptography key accurately. The screen turns green after the guard's finished. An invisible door appears within the shell of this incubator. A rectangular opening grants access to the room. The door had been invisible before it opened, its frame dissolved into the outer wall. Opening, the cells separated and slid down, a science I haven't seen before. I wonder if it would work on Earth the same way, or if it's unique to this planet.

"Yesha, these are your quarters. You'll find your belongings and issued items inside. The glass has ultraviolet protection so feel free to view the solar eclipse at ease."

Yesha steps carefully from the car and into the incubator. She looks at me with wide eyes before the frosted door resumes its place, and I'm unable to see her except for her shadow, hands pressed against the glass. We move forward and upward. When we stop again, we're close to the top of the hill.

"Vienna, this is your stop."

"Thanks." I don't know why I said it. The guards haven't been kind, but this one seems less forceful. There's something alluring about him that I can't pinpoint. As I step into my own incubator and look back to watch him leave, I notice a look of surprise on his face.

"Well, night then," he says with a grunt and zooms off, back to the rest of the group. I'm actually able to see him the entire way, even though the door has closed. While the glass appears frosted from the outside, it's clear as air from within.

I look up and can see the beautiful sky. I can see the cliff from an adjacent hill. I take a seat on the rock floor and view the solar eclipse in silence. My heart slows down in this solitary confinement. I'm finally able to relax a little. When I look down, I gasp at the height. The clear bubble makes it feel as if I would fall after one step forward. Since I'm sitting on rock solid ground, I reach my foot out and tap the globe. It's there, but without touching it, I'd never know.

I turn around and take in my new home. There's a metal lavatory on the right with a sink, small shower, and a commode for bathroom needs. On the left is a chest of three drawers with my mom's purse on top. I turn a full circle, but do not find a bed or chair anywhere. Where am I supposed to sleep? The sense that I should be in hand and ankle shackles resurfaces inside this cell. That's what it is, nothing more than a jail cell. While there had been a holographic screen on the outside for entry, I don't see one in here. I try opening the door but it's securely locked. The glimmer of hope about this difficult place is crushed as if an avalanche came down the hill right on top of me. The blockade of hills emanates beyond our incubators. They blend in with the ground except they wear stern masks as if they have on armor. A rock cascades down one followed by silence. A moon appears behind a hill and the hill takes on a new life. It's pointed peaks like wolf fangs. I'm surrounded by the things of nightmares. How am I going to save Dad, wherever he is?

I open Mom's purse and find the extra lab coat and identification card. I hug the purse close to me as I open the drawers. The first one has six lab coats perfectly folded with a note on top. I instantly remember the note that brought me here. The note I hold now doesn't have a code behind the text. It's plain and simple English, typed not handwritten. It says we are only to wear issued lab coats going forward. We may keep the ones we brought with us to wear only in our quarters. It also states the contents of the other drawers: pajamas, one mat, bottles of water, undergarments, six pairs of slacks, toiletries, and a foldable tablet for journaling. It goes on to say we'll be issued fitted boots tomorrow.

The pants are in the second drawer and the other items in the third. I take the pajamas out. They're a long sleeve button-up shirt and pants, beige with lines of blue. Not exactly the most fashionable, but I'm alone so who cares.

I grab the pajamas and the toiletry bag and head to the metal lavatory. I close the door, even though no one can see in. It just feels weird to change while I can see out in the open. The pajamas fit perfectly. They must've used my body measurements from my identification. Brushing my hair and teeth in front of the mirror is like I'm making this my home, which is odd.

I can't help but stare out into this planet's land. Being in one of the highest incubators gives me a view beyond the wall. Far off, I can see the perfect shape of a cactus. It's taller than the ones on Earth and the branches curve at the ends in a way unlike any cacti I have ever seen. The cacti here are like the Red Wood trees on old Earth, enormous in person and yet a speck of dust in the universe. It's strange to see with the sun peeking around a moon as the backdrop. Hope fills me with the sight of these exquisite, boomerang shaped leaves. I unroll the mat and lie down. My head is on a rock. I take my dad's old lab coat and roll it under my head. As I stare out, I begin to notice other incubators' lights turning off. I'm not ready for night. As I lie there, a memory floods my thoughts.

Dad always saved one science experiment just for me. He didn't share it with my mom or any of his colleagues. Like Einstein, he enjoyed smaller experiments outside of his main career. One experiment that intrigued Einstein also intrigued my dad. I remember him showing it to me when he found I was afraid of the night in the desert. It was of a radiometer, a mini-windmill type contraption, that spun one way under the sun and at night, in the dark, spun the other direction. It'd been enough to distract me and allow me to fall asleep at ease. Before long, I was no longer afraid of the night. As I turn and sense an ache in my hip where a rock had been pressing, I wish I had his windmill contraption now. I wonder if my baby brother is afraid of the desert night too.

I stand up and notice almost every other light is off. When I search for the switch to shut my own off, I find exposed pipes on both sides of the room. Since it's only six feet wide, an idea begins to formulate in my head. I use my lab coats, the clothes I'd been wearing, and the purse. As I tie everything together and to the pipes, I step on my mat. It has a rod at each end. There are nail clippers minus a file in the toiletry bag. I use them to partially remove the rods from the mat. As I place the rods between the sleeves tied to each pipe, the mat sets on top of my work. I take a step back. Pretty discombobulated, but it should suffice.

Lying on the makeshift hammock is much more comfortable. It kind of feels like I aced an assessment. I find the switch next to one of the pipes. Now that my lights are off, and no rock protrudes into my body, I'm finally able to drift off to sleep.

A beeping sound chimes over and over again.

I say, "Snooze," and roll over. The harsh slap of my body hitting the rock floor fully awakens me.

As I search my body for any broken skin, a voice fills the incubator. "Vienna, your escort will arrive in twenty minutes."

I look up and find an intercom in the ceiling to be the source of the voice. Twenty minutes isn't a long time, so I grab the toiletries and issued clothing. The pain in my hip, as I enter the lavatory, leads me to believe I'll have a pretty bruise within the next couple of hours. What a way to begin the first lab day. The facility issued lab coat's stiff when I put it on. It's nothing like the comfort and warmth of Dad's old coat. When exactly twenty minutes have passed, the door to my incubator magically slides open. Feverish heat engulfs my room with the sunlight. Last night, I hadn't paid attention to the canopy above the rails. In the day, I'm grateful for it. Stepping outside, I see the same guard who dropped me off last night. In the light, he's even more unique. Unlike the others, his eyes are close together and nose not quite so large.

"Morning," I say.

He extends his hand and assists me onto the railcar.

He peers into my room as I board. "Nice hammock you put together there." I'm not sure, but I think I see his cheeks expand from behind. Could he be smiling?

We pick up Yesha, and she looks groggy.

"What's with the lack of beds and only a bloody rock floor as a substitute?" she asks.

"I built a hammock. Want me to build one for you too?"

"You're not allowed within one another's quarters. She'll have to build it herself," the guard says.

"Well, I just used my personal stuff, the exposed pipes, and the mat rods. I can try to email you a multidimensional prism photo with the foldable tablet."

"No, email isn't allowed. Rules stipulate it in order to preserve the privacy of experiments and reduce the possibility of corruption. Oh, and don't let Rigled hear about those rods."

"Are we allowed to do anything here?" Yesha asks. "Is

Rigled the one with the scratchy voice? Man gets miffed at the slightest."

"Best to follow the rules. Makes life a lot easier around here. Yeah, that's him," the guard answers.

"What's *your* name?" I ask.

"Colsam, but don't address us by name in public. We're supposed to keep to our own kind here."

'Colsam' seems fitting. Wholesome Colsam! I *am the biggest dork ever!* Why is there such separation? The guards seem to be everywhere we go. So, why can't we talk to them? Again, the penitentiary sensation returns.

All the newbies are fitted with boots as if we're part of a military drill team. Yesha and I have the same size boot, which I try to point out to her, but she seems focused on studying the facility. After that, Rigled escorts us to a classroom, another perfectly square room with rounded corners.

Upon arrival, I'm surprised to see others in attendance. People who aren't new to the facility sit in some of the chairs. I spot Al and his conifer scent first. It's hard to turn away from his malachite eyes but I look to see if he has the same boots that we just received and notice his ankles are bionic like his right hand. He notices my eyes gazing and lowers the pant cuffs with his left hand to cover the bionic limbs. I can't help the jaw drop when I realize his left hand is bionic too. He quickly looks in the other direction. I shake my head to steady myself. The seat next to him is open. I approach.

"Is anyone sitting here?"

"Na, but you don't have to if it makes you feel uncomfortable."

I take the seat. "I'm not uncomfortable. I was just surprised. It's not every day that someone with four bionic limbs catches me."

"Does someone catch you daily?" he asks with a playful smile. I can't help but smile back while I shake my head no.

"Is this the one from the cafeteria?" the artery man who caused me to stumble in the cafeteria asks. And my jaw drops yet again. He's sitting to Al's left. I notice Yesha gives him a wide berth as she passes to take the open seat next to me. Despite the arteries that I can see pulse and his strong stature, I notice the dimples below his eyes as he speaks.

"That's me. I'm Vienna. What's your name?"

"It's Viscerous. Glad to meet you." He extends his hand for a shake, and I don't hesitate. It feels as though worms wiggle between our hands, but the shake's warm, and he has one of the biggest smiles I've ever seen. He and Al tilt their heads in approval after the shake. "You have a firm shake there."

"Thanks."

A video displays on a holograph screen at the front of the room for our course. Most of the information is stuff I already know. Proper lab experiment techniques, sanitary procedure, and toxic waste bins are among the topics. I catch Yesha yawning out of the corner of my eye. When the course discusses my assigned lab, I sit up taller. Our next assignment will be non-bio bodies that have implanted memory and conscience. When that section finishes, Al whispers to me.

"Are you in the blood and body diagnostics lab too?"

"Yeah, are you?"

He nods. My heart skips a beat. Al's already caught me from falling. Knowing that we're going to be lab mates gives me hope and makes me nervous at the same time. Perhaps he can help me find my dad. I'm probably getting ahead of myself, but I can't help the bubble that floats through me. It's like right before giving a speech, a euphoric and pre-cliff-jumping high.

All of the sudden the screen's gone blank like an indoor solar eclipse. I'm afraid one of the guards caught our hushed conversation. A new guard enters, approaches the teacher, and whispers something. I don't like the secretive process. It's dark, cold, and unnerving.

"Excuse me, class, change of plans. Please take a fifteen-minute break and then head to your assigned labs."

We all look at each other, unsure of what to do.

Then the guard looks at Lucretia. "You, stay here."

I try to read her face to decipher what's going on. Should I stay with her? Yesha leans over and whispers in my ear, distracting me.

"Now's a good time to check out the tunnels. You memorized those blueprints, right?"

I hope our whispers are more nonchalant than the guards'.

"I think so."

"Bloody hell. I'll take the North wing. You know which direction's south?"

I should know this but being on another planet's disorienting. Yesha tilts her head.

"Yeah, got it," I lie.

We all leave, and I try to remember where the access to the South tunnel is. Luckily, I hid the blueprints in my undergarments despite Yesha's instructions to memorize and destroy.

When I'm in a quiet hallway, I pull out the blueprints. The South entrance isn't too far. I bet Yesha picked the North because it was further away and would be more difficult. If I go right from the entrance, I can go over the room we just left. It's risky because they might hear me, but I have to see why they kept Lucretia behind. When I'm at the entrance vent, I look both ways, glad to see the coast is clear. I quietly remove the metal vent cover, crawl into the tunnel, and replace the cover.

The tunnel is made of a strong plastic, which is good. My crawling would be much louder in a metal tunnel. It's dark and hard to see. I attempt an army crawl but move very slowly. I stop every so often to listen for any sounds indicating that someone's heard me. My hands shake the entire way. But I have figured out where the watermelon smell was coming from. I smell it stronger here than I have anywhere else before.

And then, I run into something! I reach my hand forward and touch the tread of a boot. Whose boot? My breath quickens. The boot moves and I gasp. I can't help it. Whoever it is rolls to their side and then there's light. I'm blinded by the change. Oh no! I'm found! This is someone working on maintenance. I shouldn't be here. What's going to happen? As my eyes adjust, I see that's it's Al. He has a flashlight. He holds his finger in front of his mouth. Yes, I can be quiet if the pounding in my chest would only stop. Then he motions for me to move forward, next to him. An invitation? He's not mad. He doesn't care that I'm here. When I'm next to him, he softly places his hand on the side of my face, slightly turning my head toward another vent cover.

It's in front of and below us and looks into the room with Lucretia. He once again motions for silence and I nod my head. The same guards stand beside Lucretia. Everything's the same as when we left. What have they been doing this whole time?

Then the door opens and Quintus, the man who'd been escorted from the cafeteria, enters. As the doctor who choked joins Lucretia in the computer lab, she pivots her chair toward him. She begins to say something to him, but he shakes his head no. The dark circles around his eyes make him look as though he hasn't slept for days. His eyes are bloodshot like he's consumed too much alcohol the previous day or something. What's happened to him? Lucretia rises to help him into a chair.

"You're not to approach," Rigled says to her.

"Look at him. He needs someone's help."

She continues her way to him as if gravity pulls her that way instead of down, but the guards surround her and begin flogging her with chain whips, the skin tearing from her body and her blood spilling to the floor. My heart's pounding so hard I find it difficult to breathe, the way you feel right after you barely miss a head-on collision. I contemplate throwing the vent cover at them like a lethal frisbee. I look at Al. His hands are in fists and his jaw muscle keeps tensing. Lucretia's arm, back, and even part of her face are being shredded. I have to do something.

I'm about to jump out of the tunnel and attack with my bare hands when Quintus lunges toward the guards, only to be burned by a guard's flame-throwing club. What in the world? No! This cannot be happening. The guard looks away and holds his weapon at a distance. Quintus jumps back startled and then drops to the floor, extinguishing the flames in his hair and clothes. I want to go to him but find myself in a sudden state of paralysis. As the smell of burnt hair permeates the area, I want to retch, but I haven't consumed anything in the past day. The image of him burning and her skin peeling away will haunt me forever. I begin to reach for the vent cover to fight the demons who did this, the urge for revenge over-coming my paralysis, but a hand on my shoulder stops me. When I look at Al, his head's down, and I see a tear dropping off his cheek.

"You two are traitors and this is what happens to traitors here," Rigled yells.

It's as if I'm floating, and the vent's not really there. Some of the staff enter and take the pair out of the classroom on gurneys for medical treatment. My eyes watch them rolled out as the images sear into my brain. I find it very difficult to breath. Will they be okay? Why did this happen?

Al grabs my hand, and I feel as though I've returned to my body but when he talks to me, I'm unable to hear. Al begins crawling back the way I came, and I follow him. I'm afraid to leave the tunnel. Al has a tiny mirror and he pokes it out of the vent to be sure no one's around. We exit and I'm kind of grateful to no longer be crammed in a tunnel, but I'm over-whelmed with insecurity and exposure. Walking is like tramping through mud. My boots get heavier with each step. I don't see the labs that we walk by; the activity within them blurs past us as if we're travelling at light speed. All I'm able to focus on is skin hanging like drapes off a bone or melting away to expose the muscle beneath. I know we're walking in a straight line, but it feels as if I'm spinning. I stumble and fall. Al picks me up and carries me the rest of the way in his bionic arms. I stare at his eyelashes that reach for the sky, attempting to block out the gruesome visuals in my mind.

As I enter my assigned lab for the first time, I'm grateful the hallway wall isn't full of windows, just round shapes. I want protection from what I witnessed. Al sets me down on a chair, and Viscerous brings a blanket, wrapping it around me. Its warmth dispels the lonely coldness, like the isolation astro-nauts had to endure after their long lunar trips almost two centuries ago.

Then, Viscerous speaks to a woman who'd been sitting on his left during the course. I hadn't even noticed her before. "Grab her a glass of water, Albina. She's in a state of shock."

My hearing is returning. As Albina leaves, fills a glass, and returns, I notice her name fits her looks, a welcome diversion. She has light skin, almost so clear that her arteries appear to be outside of the skin like Viscerous'. Her eyes are gray with a blue tint. It's as if she's a ghost floating in front of the sterile, smooth surfaces of the lab. I can't help but stare as she hands me the glass. I want to say thank you, but my mouth is as dry as a desert. I slowly take a sip of the water.

"She'll be fine," Albina says with a nod of approval.

"What happened?" asks Viscerous.

"They brought Quintus into the classroom and it was bad," Al says.

"What is Cromwell thinking?" Viscerous asks.

"We better be careful. I've always said that one runs his mouth too much," Albina says. "Wait, they did this in front of everyone?"

"It wasn't just Quintus. They hurt Lucretia," Al says.

"Where were you?" Albina asks.

"The tunnels," Al says.

"Might need to stay away from those for a while," Viscerous says.

Albina gives me a look, raising an eyebrow as if to say, "And how did you find the tunnels?"

"I'm so tired of this," Al interrupts.

He picks up an Airblow, an umbrella that uses air pressure to keep sand out of your eyes, and marches to the side of a cement wall hidden from the door's view. That's when I notice the dozens of scrolled tallies on the wall like markings in a jail cell. It seems I cannot escape the imprisonment here. The markings appear to be a count of some sort, but what could they be for? He points the Airblow at the wall, and as he marks two new tallies, I realize it's been amped up enough to penetrate cement.

"What are you doing?" My voice has returned, a surprise not just to Albina, Viscerous, and Al. I hold my hand against my vocal cords to be sure it was me that spoke.

"Look, she's alive," Viscerous says, moving like a robot, his arms held out in front of him as he walks.

"I'm making marks for those abused here," Al says.

He's journaling Cromwell's crimes and injustices publicly. There are so many tallies. It doesn't seem possible. Quintus and Lucretia's experience will live forever in the cement, a biography of the abused. I think of the doctors who were just ripped apart and burned. The only reason I can find to explain why this happened is their conversation aboard the shuttle. I hear Lucretia's voice clearly in my head, "He's watching even now." I run up to the wall and begin rubbing the markings as if I can somehow make them disappear.

"He's watching us. What do you think he'll do if he sees this?" I ask.

"He doesn't here. Our findings are to be kept secret from everyone, even the guards." Albina says. "He only receives the daily reports we issue him from here."

Viscerous puts his hand on my shoulder, easing me from the headstone.

"Everything's okay, Vienna," Al says.

"Who is this Cromwell guy, anyway? He seems to have everyone else do his harm for him. I don't think I've seen him once," I say. "And, why would you really think he's not watching here?"

"Um, yeah, you did. Don't you remember? He's the one who had Quintus removed from the cafeteria."

I was that close to my dad's kidnapper and I didn't even realize it. What a jerk! He made an announcement in the cafeteria as if nothing was wrong, all the while planning to do horrible things to Quintus.

I stand up from the wall and nervously wring the end of my coat.

"Will Quintus and Lucretia be okay?"

They all raise their eyebrows. Then Al speaks, "I think they'll be all right. We have a drove of medical abilities here. One of the few benefits."

"What else goes on here?" I ask.

"Pretty much whatever Cromwell comes up with. How'd you think I acquired my bionic limbs?"

I'm glad to hear Lucretia and Quintus should be fine, but the oxygen is knocked out of me when I learn Al's reason for artificial limbs. I sit right there on the floor. Cromwell has done this to them, what has he done to Dad?

"How do you think my arteries came to be outside the epidermis?" Viscerous asks.

"What do you think caused my absence of pigmentation?" Albina asks as she clasps her arm around Viscerous.

"You all have been mutated! But why?" I ask as black spots encroach my vision. My limbs begin to feel as if they're made of concrete and a sea of darkness threatens to wash over me.

6

FIELD TRIP

Vienna

"Dr. Cromwell wanted to see how limb, artery, and pigment transplantation would work. If different parts could perform together to form a new body," Al answers my question, but I still don't understand. Why run these studies on doctors? He's holding my head in his strong hands and looking at me concerned. I swear I can feel his pulse against the back of my neck but that can't be right. It must be my own.

"But why?" I ask. I mean, I understand wanting a unified management, but this is dictatorship. I believe unified management saved Earth from total annihilation, but if you completely strip intelligent beings from decision-making, you're only asking for revolt. We can't survive with our hands tied behind our backs. I believe people have a need to prove themselves. How can they do that in a situation that binds them with such brute force?

"Don't ask me," Viscerous answers. "Cromwell's studies

seem to be for a useful purpose of some sort, but we don't receive clearance to learn what, even when he takes our physical and most useful traits."

"The man has no end to the liberties he takes," Albina relents.

Al looks at the clock on the wall. "Think you're up to some scientific studies? If we don't fill the schedule report, it'll only raise questions."

I have to take a deep breath in to fully understand what's taking place. Anything to take my mind off of what just happened and the things I'm finding out. I stand up and grab a pair of latex gloves from the nearest table.

"All you have to do is study the previous blood, muscular, memories, and psychological presence of the human body for one study," Al says. "Think you can manage that with everything that's gone on?"

Of course, please distract me with work. "Yeah."

"You won't be needing those gloves," Al says as he taps on one of the holographic screens. The image of a woman comes up. "You've been assigned to Charlie. She's a non-bio body with the memories and conscience of a deceased human body. Right now, if you study the lab results of the human body, it will prepare you for meeting Charlie next lab."

"I'm going to meet her next time I'm here. I've never met a non-bio."

"It'll help if you're completely familiar with the results. I have my own results to review. You really going to be okay?"

"Yeah, yeah." I begin reviewing while Al, Viscerous, and Albina start their own tasks. It appears their ability to perform these tasks didn't prevent them from being used in experiments. I'd hoped my ability in the lab would prolong my time, but now I'm full of inquisitiveness and a thought crosses my mind.

"What made Cromwell choose you for transplantation experiments?" I ask all of them.

"The high platelet count within my blood gives more stability to my veins and arteries, so Cromwell found me perfect for an arterial transplant experiment."

"So, do you still have your own arteries, or do those belong to someone else?"

"These are mine. The other subject didn't survive the movement of his bloodlines."

I'm unable to ask more. Someone died because of these experiments. It's as if the Oath to Preserve Life never existed here. I have to take a deep breath before I can talk.

"I'm sorry, Viscerous. I'm glad you survived."

"I only survived because Septimus was able to suture vital connections in time. He couldn't handle two of us simultaneously. He'd argued with Cromwell to allow the procedures to be done separately. If Cromwell would have listened, death could've been avoided."

I hope he didn't see my eyes widen at the mention of my dad's name. Of course, my dad would have been able to save them both. It sounds like even under these conditions, he's attempting to keep his oath intact. How could I ever have doubted him?

"Septimus is the one who kept me alive during my procedure too," Al says. "I could tell he didn't want to be part of the entire thing, but since he was forced to partake, he decided to at least protect the lives of the subjects."

Tears sting my eyes as I ask, "Who's Septimus?"

"Oh, Dr. Perierat has been here longer than most of us. Dr. Cromwell uses him as his right hand," Al says. "We all call Dr. Perierat by his first name, Septimus, because he tries to save us. I don't even think he'd be here if he had a choice. I bet Cromwell's holding something over him, otherwise I don't think he'd ever have come here. If it weren't for Septimus, there'd be more markings on that wall."

Now I begin to cry quietly and try to hide it as I continue analyzing Charlie's lab studies. When I wipe my tears away with the sleeve of my coat, Al puts a hand on my shoulder.

"What's wrong?"

"I can't tell you. It would put you and others in danger. I should've found a different way."

I just nod my head, but we make eye connection and I swear he can see right through me. It would be too dangerous to tell Al that Septimus is my dad or to tell him my real name and purpose here. I really should've found a different way to save Dad, but how was I to know about all of this? Al goes back to his studies after gently rubbing my shoulder. I need a new plan, but right now, I'm only able to focus on the task at hand. I need to keep my mind straight.

Charlie's lab results are so beautiful that they remarkably allow me to escape to the peaceful world of scientific study that I know. Thank goodness because I'm not sure how much more I can take. I have spontaneous energy findings from electroencephalography. I'm able to memorize them and distract myself. When it's time to go to dinner, not that I'm able to eat, and we head to our separate quarters, my head's still spinning with the new information. I'm closer to my dad but feel further away. At least I know he's alive and well. I have confirmation that he's here even though I've yet to see him.

––––––

On the way to the cafeteria I excuse myself so I can find Yesha. I can only imagine what she saw in the tunnels. Hopefully nothing worse. I don't know if I could handle more bad news right now. She's smiling when she exits her lab.

"Hey, you look like you're having fun."

"Oh, hey, yeah."

"What's got you in such a good mood?"

She's still smiling as we walk the halls.

"They have blinding arterial techno-bots here."

"For real?"

"Yeah, we got to see it live."

"Thought you were going to be focused solely on technology. I didn't know you'd see blood. Maybe our roles got reversed."

"You're jealous."

"No…" I'm about to tell her that right now I'm worried, not jealous. I want to ask about the tunnels but then she'll ask what I saw. I have to warn her, but it feels like I'd be breaking her current bubble. Crashing on her, it's my fault she's here. How do I tell her?

I don't get a chance to talk. I didn't realize it, but we wound up down one of the halls leading to a deep Brunswick colored door. One of the ones we don't have access to, with a pair of guards in front. They're too busy with the body they're holding by the arms to notice us. It's Pixie, the statistician! They turn her arm over to inspect her forearm. One of the guards pulls out a black light and shines it on her. I gasp, even though I know what I'm going to see…an invisible ink tattoo! Pixie was one of the ones marked on the ship. The guards turn their heads our direction when they hear my gasp.

"Don't mind her, she's numpty. It's why she led us down the wrong hall. Sorry to bug you," Yesha tells the guards as she turns me around.

I can hear my heartbeat in my ears again as we walk out of the hallway and back to the main one. Yesha has to hold onto my arm and direct me. She's looking at me as if I've just sprouted horns. I keep waiting for one of the guards to run up and knock us out, like they must have done to Pixie. Will they do to us what they did to Lucretia? Yesha puts her arms around my shoulders to comfort me.

When we turn, out of the hallway, I take a deep inhalation, not realizing I'd been holding my breath. The pounding in my ears begins to fade.

"What was that?" Yesha asks.

And so, in a deep whisper, I finally tell Yesha. I tell her about the tattoos and Pixie. I tell her about Lucretia and Quintus. I tell her about Al, Viscerous, and Albina. I release everything I've been holding in since we got here and find that I'm the one to put my arm around her shoulders now. When we arrive at the cafeteria, we can no longer talk. We have to go in to adhere to schedule, especially after the guards saw us in the wrong hall. Yesha and I eat in silence. She seems to be eyeing everyone, looking at it all differently now that she knows. When she looks at Viscerous again, knowing what's been done, she stares in anger.

When we line up at the red door this time, it's with everyone from the facility. We're given another pill and lined up in pairs. I'm next to Yesha. She didn't speak all meal. She looks lost but not completely beaten down.

"Thank you, for earlier," I say.

"No worries at all chap, but what in the hell is with this place? What they're doing is illegal. Why haven't the authorities intervened?"

I swear every muscle in her body flexes as she asks me this. She asks a good question. I need to find out how Cromwell's getting away with all of this. If I can somehow get word to the authorities, perhaps I can free my dad, no, not just Dad. *Everyone* here should not have to deal with this abuse.

"You're right, Yesha."

Rigled speaks to the group then, and our conversation is brought to an end. "We're passing out policies and procedures. You may have overheard that we have two traitors in this facility. Their sentences were pronounced, and punishment took place. Read the procedures in your quarters so they have your full attention and we don't have a repeat of today."

No one talks. No one asks for details. It's like this is a common occurrence. Some hands shake and I hear paper flutter.

As Yesha and I step outside, I notice Al is five rows in front of us. He looks back at me, and then yawns. At the end of his yawn, his hand slyly points to the hill opposite mine. Al mouths "that's Septimus, the one who saved me." When I look in the direction he pointed, I see my dad aboard a hover bike-car. *I see my dad!* My stomach feels as though it lifts to my chest. I want to jump up and down and hug everyone here, even Rigled. But I can't do any of that. His hair's grown past his ears and he now has facial hair. Mom would never approve but I don't care. He's alive, I've seen it with my own eyes. The changes in his appearance don't matter. I would recognize his crooked nose and investigating hazel eyes anywhere.

As I follow his hover bike-car, I see it stop, and he steps into his incubator. Then, I swear he looks back, right at me before the door shuts. Hints of resignation and then fear brushed across his face before it was gone. I'm finally able to see him again, yet he's imprisoned. I don't know the passcode to his incubator. I don't know which lab he's been held in all this time. If I make it known that I'm his daughter, will that put him in danger? How far would they go? They seem to have no boundaries.

As Yesha and I board with Colsam, I'm determined. I'm so close to my goal, yet it's as if achieving that goal may be impossible. It's time for me to step it up. Yesha doesn't talk until we're at her place.

"We'll figure something out, Vienna."

"Night." It's hard to say more than that right now but I'm grateful for her words.

As we leave Yesha's quarters, I can't help myself, "Colsam, do you know about everything that goes on here?" The question has plagued my mind all day. Part of me wants to like Colsam, but not if he's like the guards that can do such horrific things. I didn't see him with Lucretia, and I didn't see him with Pixie. So, what was he doing?

"I find ways, uh, around many of the responsibilities I don't agree with here, but don't tell anybody that. They wouldn't like it if I was talking to any of you."

"Why are you here?"

"You really want to know?"

"Yes, the guards, beings from your planet, seem to follow directives here without question. Why is that?"

"Trust me, most of us don't want to follow orders but, with Cromwell's involvement in the World Government, we're unable to question anything."

"But you're so strong. You could squash most of us like bugs."

"Uh, yeah, I guess that's how you'd see it."

I think I see him blush before he continues.

"This is my home planet. Things were very different before Cromwell took over about a decade ago."

"What was it like back then?"

"Fellow Vortexians had freedom. We openly discuss differing political beliefs and each side respected the other. But then our economy failed. We experienced what you refer to as a depression."

"I'm sorry to hear that, Colsam."

"Cromwell presented numbers that would turn our deficits around, and they have, but at what cost? Everyone backs his scientific studies, but few witness the results. I hope to someday return my home to what it once was, freeing fellow citizens."

"But Cromwell is only the head of the medical facility. Aren't there other places you could work?"

"He's got connections with our government too. Keep your friends close and your enemies closer, right?"

What does he mean by that? Uh, we're out of time. Rigled's motioning for Colsam to return.

"Right. Night, Colsam."

"Night, Vienna."

With that, he's speeding off to take everyone else to his or her places. I look across at my dad's incubator and can see his shadow moving about. *I can see my dad moving!* So many moments growing up I yearned to have him tuck me in and read me a book. So many times when I saw my mom sitting alone watching projected visual and sound transmissions, I wished for him to be sitting next to her. And, now he's here, impossible to retrieve but here. I'm happy and I'm torn. So many things have happened in one day!

Taking the issued lab coat off feels like removing an asylum vest. To wear scrubs has been a dream of mine for years. People look at those in scrubs as saviors they can run to in an emergency. As I put the coat down, I notice that these scrubs keep the shape in which they were starched and ironed, as if they march to their own beat. They want to stay in the form they'd been forced into instead of contouring to my body.

I'd like to sense normalcy in some way on this alien planet, but not even my clothes are willing to help me out. These scrubs are a sure sign we'll be studying medical revelations and game changers. Nevertheless, this uniform gives us a unified finding. Only a few miraculous discoveries that could resuscitate lives will see the light of day here. These are just another part of Cromwell's imprisonment. How many shackles can the man come up with? The focus here isn't on an epiphany that'll conquer disease or win a Nobel Prize. We'll only bring about more harm. Even without the straitjacket, I feel as if my arms are strapped across my chest.

I try to sleep, but I'm too afraid to turn off my lights even though homesickness has tired me out. The pictures of the two abused in the classroom infiltrate my mind. After that, all I am able to envision are images of Albina, Viscerous, and Al being mutated. Then my mind reels and I remember Pixie. I know another passenger received an invisible ink tattoo. Who was it? What could be happening to them? I read some of the policies and procedures, hoping to tire myself and avoid penalties, but that doesn't work. I look out on the planet, hoping something will soothe me to sleep. I see movement in the desert beyond. Something circles with wings spread out. I see it pause and then dive after something. Great, it's a vulture with the wing-span as long as a poli-magno. As if I need any more fuel for the nightmares I'm fighting off.

I look out to where my dad's incubator is and see he has a symbol against his glass. It's his fist with the thumb, pointer, and pinkie raised, sign language for *I love you*. I don't know how long he's had it up there. I go to my own glass and hold my hand up the same way. His lights go out, and I turn off mine. He's given me the peace I need to sleep with only a few fingers raised. That's my dad, the one who should've been with me all the years of my childhood. It's as if all the tucking in's and reading of books were merged into that one symbol. It's something I can carry with me always.

When the alarm tolls, I've only slept a couple hours, but I wake with a sense of purpose. No matter how bad this place may be, every scientific finding has a few deviations. I just need to focus in order to find them. First, how can I find a way to communicate with Dad? I wonder if we could sign an entire message the way we did last night. Second, how can I communicate with other officials not linked with Cromwell and actually get intervention? At least I have starting points, but there's still a lot of work and planning to be done. I scarf down break-fast as if I haven't seen food in days, which in all honesty, my stomach hasn't. My consumption of "I don't care what" is interrupted by the arch-nemesis.

"Good fellows of the facility, an asteroid hit Planet Vortex last night. It's quite a few miles out, but we need to approach it and collect water. Many studies show that it would take years for the water from an asteroid to make it to the surface. Luck-ily, with the Vortex moons, it only takes hours. Will any of you volunteer for this venture? You know, exploration is good for the mind."

Did the asteroid hit during my short period of sleep? I don't remember feeling any tremors. Al's hand shoots up. I see Viscerous and Albina also raise theirs. Without hesitation, my hand lifts from my body too. Anything to be away from this place and clear my thoughts sounds good about now. Surpris-ingly, Yesha raises her hand as well. I'd assumed she'd be so intrigued by the lab studies she wouldn't want to leave. Yester-day's happenings must have shaken her more than I realized. Al shrugs his shoulders at me. Guess he'll be teaching me more about this place. I don't understand why Cromwell wouldn't just send some guards for this mission. I wonder if it's an evaluation.

"Wonderful, you five will be paired up with a couple guards," Cromwell says as he points to Rigled and one I only recognize as the operator of the flame-throwing club from yesterday, great. Not exactly who I'd nominate as our escort on this mission. If only Colsam could help us out.

We exit the cafeteria to a place I've never been. It's like a shuttle airlock room filled with equipment to prepare a voyager for a foreign environment. I half expect to see a wheel handle for exit, but there isn't one that I can see. The guards size us for backpacks equipped with water bag pouches and suits that will protect us from the elements. As the guards leave to collect the appropriate sized packs, Viscerous begins informing Yesha and me about the planet's dangers and a feeling of spiders crawling up my skin begins.

"On Planet Vortex, there are vultures that can kill you with just one beak plunge. You must stay out of their sight if you want to survive. I've seen a couple of the guards attacked by them.

"With its many moons and orbit path around the sun similar to Earth's, most of the time you'll be fine. If you see a spot like one a child makes with a magnifying glass on Earth but bigger, you'll be burnt to a crisp instantly. I've concluded that the lower gravity and condensation in the cloud pools cause a large curvature width. It's amazing how the multiple moons extract the minimal groundwater causing clouds in what would appear as an impossible environment."

"What protective weapons will we be issued?" Yesha asks, looking around for electronic shields or drone guinea pigs.

Al, Viscerous, and Albina all give each other looks and say, "None," at the same time. This has definitely got to be a freaking test.

I see Yesha's eyes widen, but she doesn't protest. I wonder where Yesha's strength stems from. She questioned processes from the get-go and thought about government alliance. Yet again, I'm yearning to get her closer. And the question of why she was so against this planet from the beginning has me wondering still.

When the guards escort us outside, I'm not completely surprised by the hover-bikes free of rails. They seem to be heavier than those we have at home. Since there are five of us, Al and Viscerous pair with the flame-throwing club guard. That leaves Yesha, Albina, and I with Rigled. Yesha and I agree to share a seat. I want to be close to her, but not this close.

As we hover off into this planet's desert, I notice that the sand billows out and upward. When shaded, the hills take on a blood-like color, but in the light of the sun they seem gray. The heat causes all hydration to cook off me. I can see a vapor cloud from it. I'm grateful for the backpacks as I take a sip from the connecting straw. Once we're close enough, we make the rest of the journey on foot. Rigled says we could contaminate the water supply if we fly too close to it with all our weight on board, so he'll send the other guard back to the hover after he has perfect coordinates to send via flexible tablet in order to make the proper landing. Appears guards are able to email each other freely even though scientists are not.

During our trek through the desert, I notice the blue sky is similar to that on Earth, apart from the two moons I can see in midday. Multiple moons offer a constant shadow duplication like sunlight shooting rainbows through prisms. The clouds paint the sky on Vortex just like Earth except more like paint splotches or sparkler flares littering the sky instead of cotton candy. The clouds are puffier and closer than at home. It feels as though I could reach out and touch one.

Al begins to distance himself further from our group. We've been assigned guards, but they're more interested in their own safety than protecting us. They let us walk far beyond them.

"Should he really be venturing out so far away from us?" Yesha asks me.

"Al's stronger than you think," Viscerous answers on my behalf. "His bionic limbs have many benefits. Plus, he needs to feed his adventurous side while we're free to roam the desert instead of locked in the lab."

"Al also has a better eye than any of us," I add, "look ahead and to the left." I point at a shadowed rocky cliff just as Al slows to meet us. It's about two hundred meters out.

"See the vulture on the cliff at eleven?" Al asks us as we catch up with him.

We make our way to a small rocky point in the desert to

take cover. I keep my head up, peering around longer than is probably safe. I want to see the layout of this land even if it's hotter than a 3-D printer can be with a jam. Is this where I'll take my dad when I free him from the life-crushing medical facility? I want to see what these deadly vultures are like.

The heat bakes my face and sweat droplets pour down my cheek. I pull back in time to escape being seen by a vulture, I think. My chest begins to spasm with quick inhalations. I grab onto the sand like it can hold me down.

7

COMPANION

Vienna

"Vienna, there's a hot," Al yells at me as heat begins charring my skin, but before he can finish, talons grab my arms just below the shoulders and I instantly try to assess if my aorta is safe.

As I'm lifted in the air, I see the refracted light beam point to the spot where I'd been by the rock. It burns a hole, smoldering the rock to dust. The multidimensional prism photons within the smaller space blaze everything in its path.

If it weren't for the vulture, I'd be fried to a crisp. I'm grateful to escape the searing, but afraid of what's holding me now. I'm surprised the pointed talons aren't gouging my skin and spilling blood. The vulture's skin is dinosaur like and not just on the talons I can see, but on the thumbs pressing into my back too. I shudder at the thought, but the vulture doesn't lose me, which is good since we're fifty feet in the air. The grip doesn't even bruise, though it's strong enough to carry me. Then I realize how close I am to the beak. It could plunge into my side easily right now. Goosebumps prickle my arms even though it's hot as fire out here. The beak could stab through one side of my body and poke out the other, it's so long.

I begin to spasm with fear the way I would have if I'd been able to see the hot spot Al tried to warn me about approaching. My breaths become so fast, I'm afraid I might have a heart attack. The vulture only flies about twenty meters before descending and setting me down. I brace myself, glad to be alive and ready to bolt, but the vulture only lowers its head to my feet, bending its neck in a vulnerable way. This isn't at all what I had envisioned.

Then the vulture does something else completely unexpected. It rubs its head against my hand. Despite my consternation, I do the only thing natural when an animal shows affection this way. It did just save me. I pet it, not like a dog tousling the fur, but like a cat, stroking down so that I don't ruffle its feathers. The black eyes study me and I swear its beak opens slightly as if showing happiness. I've always wanted a pet, but Mom believes they're full of germs. I wonder if this is what it would've been like.

A snap sounds about twenty feet away. I look up to see that Rigled has released the chain whip from his belt. Luckily, the Vortex government has banned guns. I surprise myself by moving to stand between Rigled and the vulture. My brain seems void of all common sense, as if adrenaline has taken over my thoughts. Before Rigled can make another move, I hear the strong flapping and fluttering of the vulture flying off.

"Why did you interfere? I had the beast within my reach," Rigled yells at me.

"He just saved me. He wasn't going to cause any harm," I answer.

As I spot the vulture flying off, its head turns around and

issues a nasty hiss in Rigled's direction. When I turn back, I see two guards in front of me instead of one.

"You can't trust those damn birds," Rigled retorts.

"Yeah, think of what they did to Cromwell's wife and kid," the flame-throwing guard says. "The facility was a different place when they were around."

What is he talking about? I never imagined Cromwell had a family. And, he lost them…in a violent way. How awful!

"Be quiet, fool. Why don't you be useful and go get one of the hovers?" Rigled says to the guard as he slaps his mallard head and the guard retreats in the direction we left the hovers.

Al grabs my hand and Yesha grabs the other. Albina and Viscerous are shortly behind them holding each other's hands.

"Never seen anything like that before," Viscerous says.

"Don't repeat a word of this incident when we return," Rigled warns.

I think I understand now why Rigled was insistent upon attacking the vulture. Had he attacked while I was petting the bird, I probably would've been in the way. With Rigled's whip caught on me, the vulture would easily have been in a position to attack him. If vultures did cause harm to Cromwell's family and a guard let a vulture free without attacking it, what would that mean for the guard?

"All right, the water's close now," Rigled announces as his eyes follow the vulture leaving us behind by miles. "There are tanks to fill within the hovers. Get to work."

As we walk, I notice the sand isn't hot like on a baked desert but cool like near the water on a beach. I wish our family vacations had been on a beach and my dad had been just a normal guy and not a scientific success. We wouldn't be stuck on Planet Vortex. We'd be living normal lives. When we make it to the top of a dune, a mirage takes over my sight. It's a lake in the middle of the desert.

Everyone runs toward this natural artwork in glee, it

doesn't disappear when we near it, as I feared. Albina and Yesha drop to their knees and observe the water. I follow their moves and wonder how we'll purify it from the contamination of dust. Al and Viscerous stay back as if they're afraid of the water. The flame-throwing guard appears with a hover and then retreats into the desert. I watch his sand dust billow out above a crater. The sand actually hits a cloud and disperses, forming a haze in front of one of the moons.

"Take the lines from the hover and connect them to the water," Rigled orders.

We follow his command, but I find myself wondering how much the tanks can hold. Part way through the work, Rigled orders us to stop. He then pushes a button and the tank's volume meter lowers. They're altering its state so it'll take less space. Then he orders us to put the lines back into the water. The other guard returns with the second hover. After six series like this, the tanks are full. They must filter it at the facility.

"Hop on and hold tight," Viscerous tells us.

We all follow his instructions and I'm glad. The speed at which we return to the facility is like being in a poli-magno race. Even though we're going fast, I notice that we haven't seen a sign of population in the miles we've travelled. How far spaced out can the inhabitants be on this planet? Or how small are their numbers? I'd hoped there would be some residents apparent outside the facility.

When we arrive at the facility, we have to help return the water to liquid state, purify it, and put it into the facility inventory. No one utters a word. It's as if the guards have heightened security after our freedom. Back to the place of imprisonment, we return.

I see another group head out to collect more water. I also notice Yesha distancing herself from the group. As we all head our own way after lunch, I spot her heading down a different hallway than I've ever seen. It's full of holograph screens that seem to surveillance her as she moves. She should be heading to her assigned lab as I am. Where could she be going? Then the deep Brunswick green door resumes its place and I can no longer see her. She's going somewhere off limits. How'd she gain access? She and I are going to have a talk.

———

I'll be meeting a non-bio today. As I approach one of the cold, hard metallic beds in my lab, the object of today's studies greets me. She has silky brown hair and her skin's velvet smooth.

"Hi! I'm Charlie. What's your name?"

"Hey! It's nice to meet you. I'm Vienna," I say as I reach out and shake the first non-bio hand in my life. The skin is warm just like every other hand I've shook. Looking at Charlie I can't find a single trait that screams I'm not real, I'm non-bio.

"So, can you tell me a little about yourself?" I continue, hoping to hide my surprise. I apply hand sanitizer to prevent cross contamination, saving the latex gloves for later.

I activate the holographic screen that holds Charlie's medical report. As I read through it, I discover more about the deceased woman's conscience and memory implanted into Charlie's body. Her name was Carlie and her family could not come to terms with naming the host body the same. Carlie had come down with streptococcus pneumoniae meningitis. In recent years, the bacterium has evolved beyond reach of any vaccination or antibiotics. Microscopic robots were implanted into her bloodline, but it was too late. She had signed the non-bio body release while she'd been pregnant with her first child. During annual appointments, her doctors ran tests to assist in non-bio placement.

Charlie had suffered minor setbacks in the beginning as she believed herself to be Carlie due to the memories, but after adjusting, Charlie had been able to mimic Carlie's old behaviors. She's continued Carlie's educational if hippie style of parenting and successfully formed a loving relationship with Carlie's husband. As I tap the screen to the next page, I see a picture of Carlie staring back at me. I have to take a look back at Charlie. The image I see is perfectly identical. The skin doesn't fold at the joints as I'd expected but moves in the way a human body would.

"I love that I've been given a second chance at life. My babies still have their mother. My husband still has his wife. It's the miracle I'd prayed for."

I catch Charlie's last words, as I'd been absorbed in the report like oil droplets in water, but now resurface settling above.

"We need to run some tests to help our research in this procedure. Is that okay with you, Charlie?"

"Of course, anything I can do to give someone else the same benefits I received."

Now I put on the latex gloves. When I try to take the backing off the probes and apply them to Charlie the paper won't budge. Ugh, there must be some kind of trick. Charlie stares at me as I struggle. I look around embarrassed. Then, I try digging my fingernail between the paper and the sticky part, but the probe is removed from my hand before I can go further. I feel his warmth behind me and recognize his scent immediately. I can see which corner isn't stuck to the adhesive as Al easily removes the paper and gives me an incredulous look. He already makes me nervous. I smile and nod my head in thanks before he returns to his work.

Carlie had gone through tests before death, being accepting of non-bio continuation. Her willingness opened up research that wouldn't have been available in a sudden death without a signed release. I ask Charlie the same questions that'd been asked of Carlie, watching the monitors. Everything's lining up, but I'm interrupted. I overhear Dr. Cromwell speaking through a walkie-talkie to today's attending Vortex physician employed by the World Government. We don't have attending physicians every day, only on days Cromwell has special interest in our work. Good thing the attending physicians seem so engrossed in the studies that they don't seem to notice the wall of tallies. Perhaps they believe the tallies stand for successful studies.

"Are we closer to finding solutions? Bodies can only remain in cryogenic sleep for so long."

As Cromwell returns the physician's response with a slew of curses, apparently not receiving the answers he wanted, I begin new tests.

The test matches the electroencephalography report to a T. When I ask more questions though, I notice the pattern from before doesn't match the one I see now. Charlie's brain is showing signs of epilepsy, but no physical test had revealed this. As I pull up the keyboard, I remember Quintus wishing Cromwell would use non-bio bodies instead of live subjects. If Dr. Cromwell finds any doubt in non-bio hosts, he'll just turn to more living beings. My hand hovers away from the screen for a second while I debate.

I can't give Dr. Cromwell a reason to go after live hosts.

Instead of typing the findings on Charlie, I hack the system and delete the epileptic results. I'm able to read the structured query language, but part way through the screen begins to disappear. The system's located my intrusion. I must compromise the system in order to remain hidden. Once I'm able to move about freely, I find the weaknesses and enter my own language. I turn to Charlie, my heart melted iron. She has a family and I'm hiding information they could use to help her. Which is worse, the possibility of a seizure or guaranteed abuse?

"Test results are amazing, Charlie."

"I know. It's a miracle, right!" Charlie's smile makes me remember being scolded by my mother for bending the rules. I have to warn Charlie, even if there's no physical evidence of possible seizures.

"Definitely! Now, very rarely there are side effects. Please report if you ever have memory lapses, tingling in your extremities, sensitivity to light, or feelings of unexplained confusion."

"What? I was never told of any of those."

"Yeah, they're so rare, most physicians don't even mention them as the mere suggestion could act as a placebo. I doubt you'll ever experience any of these but like to cover all of the bases."

"I understand. It's really hard to believe, isn't it?"

As I walk to the cafeteria for dinner, it's as if the melted iron in my heart has dripped to my feet and cooled. Every step is a heavy one. Charlie has a family. What have I done?

Sitting next to my friends: Al, Viscerous, Albina, and Yesha, feels comforting after all we've been through. I'm surprised to even see a bandaged Lucretia and Quintus sitting together. I keep looking back at them to be sure they're real. Yesha doesn't say much during the meal and I'm tempted to ask her about her trip down to a limited access area. My thoughts are once again interrupted. It's hard to keep your focus in this place of ever-evolving terror.

I drop my fork as Pixie enters the cafeteria. Her hair is gone, with a bald head in its place. There's a crescent scar on the right side of her head. I motion to her, opening a space next to me for her to sit. She looks at me as if she doesn't remember who I am.

"Pixie, you can sit here with us, if you'd like."

"Thank you. I'm sorry, but I can't recall your name," she responds without the lisp she had when I met her aboard the shuttle.

"I'm Vienna. We met on the shuttle during the ride here."

"Oh, yeah."

I can tell by the look on her face that none of this registers with her. "You forgot to grab a drink. I can get something for you. What would you like?"

"Oh, I guess I did. I can get it. Where are the drinks?"

I point to the refrigerator of cartons and watch her walk away. She stands in front of them as if she doesn't recognize a single one.

"Looks like Cromwell has moved to brain matter transplantation," Viscerous says with a disgusted look.

The jerk actually took part of her brain! Albina had been right when she said there was no end to looking for what he wants.

I get up and head in Pixie's direction; my feet still feeling like I'm walking through drying cement. I tenderly grab her arm. "My favorite's the chocolate camel's milk, but they have succulent juices and water too."

"Thank you, I think I'll try the chocolate milk." She continues her lost stare at the cartons.

I grab a chocolate milk and hand it to her. She follows me as I walk back to the table. I fume as she takes a seat. Pixie had been a genius of a statistician. She could've told me so much about sub-conscience and conscience survival after death, but now, she can't even pick out a beverage. I no longer regret hiding negative non-bio results.

As if that wasn't enough, Cromwell stands and addresses everyone, "Not only did we discover a couple traitors within the population yesterday, but today we have a traitor among our guards, who have pledged loyalty above all else. Turning your back on loyalty is inexcusable, an act that I won't stand for."

Right after he says this, a gray mass of guards envelops Rigled at the red door. Yelling and grunts fill the area. The sounds of blows to a body make me shiver. Even though I've hated Rigled and his harsh words since my first day here, part of me is sorry when I see his knees dragging on the floor as a group of guards carries him out.

"Get your rest tonight. We'll have our first battle to the death in four years tomorrow morning," Cromwell says. This time, instead of daggers staring him down, all heads are bowed. But the eerie silence is disrupted when a few guards cheer. Not only are they abusive to us but to each other too. What drives them to such extents?

Battle to the death! It's as if the shuttle didn't take me to another planet, but another era. What are we, gladiators? Too bad I'm not a gladiator. I would use brute force to make this nonsense end. Then all of us could be free of the manacles. Someone very wise once told me to be careful what you wish!

8

TIME ALIGNMENT

Al

WATCHING VIENNA TRY TO REMOVE ADHESIVE protection strips from probes is comical. It's like she's never done it before. She must be nervous working with a non-bio for the first time. She even begins to blush. I take the probe to end her misery. As I shift on my feet our bodies touch and I feel an odd sensation. Apparently, I need to get out more. I have to walk away so I'm not stuck supervising her.

"Ah, how cute! Al to the rescue," Albina says.

"Yeah, yeah. Why don't you concentrate on your work?"

"Hit a nerve now, didn't she," Viscerous chimes in while wrapping an arm around Albina. She kisses him and then nudges him away back to his study.

I ignore them and continue but find myself looking back at her more than I'd like to admit. She engages Charlie in conversation as if they've known each other for years.

Albina interrupts my thoughts. She pulls over her data

screen so I can see the results for her non-bio body. It's awesome to see her in action. Scrolling the screen with one hand while putting a latex glove on the other. We often share data during tests to expedite the filing process at the end of a study. I look over at Viscerous. He has a set procedure. Not only are his notes clean and tidy (no extra scribbles), his work-space is spotless too. Even the gloves are set just so. I pull my screen over to his and Albina follows. And, I knock over one of his gloves. With the look he gives me I know I'll pay for my actions later. Lucky for me, we're not alone in the lab today.

"Vienna, come join us," Viscerous obnoxiously yells.

I mirror his look right back to him but don't have to worry about what Vienna thinks as she's finished her study and leaving. It's as if she's in a trance. Man, the non-bio must have shaken her more than I realized. We're going to need to help her out more than we have been. I motion her way and then give Albina a look.

"He scared her off," I say.

"That girl was in a hurry like she was running from something," Albina responds.

I give her the 'no duh' look and then point to Viscerous… who rolls his eyes. Maybe they're not parental figures…more like older siblings.

———

Colsam reminds me of a kid from the home. He's big, almost awkwardly so. He could scare anyone twice as much as Rigled, if he wanted to. But, he wouldn't harm a fly. I wonder what got him roped into this place. Anyone can see that he's not here by choice. This kid, Brian, had been the same way. We became great friends, cover for each other kind of friends.

Waiting for Colsam in the hallway bathroom near my lab was uncomfortable, good friend or not. But it was one of the few places where we could meet in private. We still had to talk in code and be very discreet if exchanging objects. He always scheduled it during times when the rest of the guards were busy. It didn't ease my nerves.

I was doing everything I could to eat up the time. I used the restroom at an extremely slow pace. Washed my hands but dropped a button. Which I then had to pick up and wash as well as my hands again. Five minutes went by, feeling like agony, until he arrived. He entered during the third hand washing.

I focus on the bulge in his sleeve as he enters. He angles his chin up as a hello of sorts. We try our best to keep it as informal as possible for the camera.

"How's the old couple?" he asks me. This was code for: have Albina and Viscerous finished their responsibilities. We have a few side projects that need attending.

"They're good, man. Still bugging the tar out of one another." My code for yes, they've completed their assigned tasks but they're growing impatient.

"I've always admired those two. Guess the only thing I could complain about would be their impatience." I nod my head but give him a look. That was a little too on the nose and not code like. He looks at his sleeve and reminds me why we're here.

I hold up the button. "Lost a button. Guess I'll need to fix my coat." I take over my lab coat setting it on the counter. Colsam picks up the cue. He grabs the side of the jacket closest to him, appearing to be inspecting it. As he inspects, he uses his other hand to remove the item from his sleeve.

"Yep, I can't help you with that, bud." And he's successfully made the delivery. I grab my jacket and exit. It takes every ounce of control to not run back to the lab. Once there, it takes more strength to keep from unrolling the maps. But, I hide them in our secret cabinet instead.

Now, if I can only figure out how to get my button back on.

———

Since I didn't get to Quintus before his trip to Earth, we haven't been able to send communication to other planets. Cromwell must know something's up. His claims that exploration feeds the mind are absolute bullshit. He's keeping us busy for a reason.

Voices slither down the tunnel in my direction as I head to his office. Gaining access via the tunnels is much easier than through the hallways below. The voices turn to bantering and scuffling sounds.

"Congratulations," it's Cromwell and he's talking to two guards in the middle of a circle of more guards. The ring of guards is cheering, slapping the pair on the back, and slamming mugs of low-gravity beer together. It's kind of messed up seeing them out of their normal regimen.

"You two are the first of many to receive Senate detail. Think of the food, fun, and scenery."

With Cromwell's words the pair in the center take turns shaking his hand and smiling bigger than I've seen any of the guards around here smile before. The clapping and laughter that had filled the tunnels abruptly stops.

"All right, time to get back to your posts," Cromwell says as he stares at the main hallway door.

The guards exit out the opposite door. One that I had not noticed before. A shadow dances across the floor as the hallway door opens and Yesha enters. She arrived at Vortex when Vienna did. How can she be having a one on one meeting with Cromwell?

"Do you have something for me?" he asks.

"Actually, to your utter surprise I'm sure, I do."

"Well don't keep me waiting. What is it?"

"Rigled talked about your family today."

Cromwell spins on his heel turning away from her. Why is she telling him? This is going to get Rigled busted in a heartbeat. He turns back to her with his fake smile.

"Did he really now?"

"Yeah, he talked about what the vulture did to them."

What? He's not the one who talked about that.

"And then, he let the vulture we ran into today free even though it abducted a scientist," she continues.

"Which scientist?"

"Oh, it was Vienna but she's okay."

Cromwell's jaw muscles tense so hard they move the skin at his temples. As he turns his head up, I see he's smiling his smile now. Why?

"Thank you for your honesty."

A government official enters next but instead of sticking around I follow Yesha. Something just does not seem right. I'm compelled to see what she's up to. She walks quickly, glancing over her shoulder many times, to an alcove in the hallway. There she pulls an old, tattered picture from her pocket. I angle my head against the vent to see the multidimensional prism photo but a noise echoes down the hall. She quickly returns it to her pocket and speeds away. I'm unable to follow her any further.

9

REUNION

Vienna

INSTEAD OF THE RAILCARS TAKING US TO THE FACILITY IN the morning, they take us to the cliff opposite my incubator. Colsam is silent the entire way. Seats surround the area for viewing.

After we've all been seated Cromwell addresses us. "The battle to the death today will be between Rigled the traitor and Marcus the brave. First, Marcus will hold battles with guards of this planet that have been sentenced to life for murder and conspiracy."

Watching Marcus in action during a few practice battles makes my nostomania return relentlessly. What's this world I've volunteered to join without reading the fine print: head surgeon puts employees in a battle to the death if they do not follow his orders without question.

Marcus isn't overbearingly large, but his carefully calculated strokes are fatal. He's ripped, but not bulky. He has a shaved head and goatee. Despite the disturbing scene, he wears a comical Mohawk of doll heads on his bald scalp like a colonial battle trophy. He reminds me of one of the characters in an online game Yesha and I used to play but this is definitely not a game. He moves like a Karate specialist: fast and deliberate. He even has an accent that makes him appear cocky as hell while those who must compete against him shake in fear. He fights well enough on his own, but give him a weapon and forget about it, done before it begins. A bowling ball rolling down the lane toward the helpless pins waiting for the collision that will take them down. He reads his opponents as well as a serial killer and targets their weaknesses within the first seconds. He could punch you in the chest and extract your heart, holding it above his head in victory *Last of the Mohicans* style.

When Rigled enters the arena, my heart breaks a little for him. I think Cromwell probably forced him into this life just like the other guards. He just had a knack for leadership. When he dodges a hit and deflects Marcus' ax, I have to keep myself from cheering. But then, Marcus' ax takes purchase in Rigled's side. The gray body doesn't fall over, but his arm grasps his side as he grabs hold of the Mohawk. When he performs a facemask type move, Marcus must take a step away. I actually have hope for Rigled until Marcus spins and his ax throw ends in Rigled's neck. The blood flows like a waterfall as Rigled drops to his knees and plummets like a timbered tree.

He won't have another heartbeat to power his assertive voice. No one but Cromwell claps when Marcus holds his hands up in victory. That's when I spot Colsam holding his hands out and bowing his head toward the other guards and facility staff. Many of them clasp their right hands in a fist on the left side of their chests. I'm glad I've made a friend in Colsam.

Everyone moves mechanically as we depart to our individual labs. Al puts his arm around my shoulders like a buddy as we make our way to our lab.

"I know it's tough, Vienna, but hang in there."

"Okay, but I'm completely lost here."

"I know." He rubs my arm, attempting to comfort me. "I know."

As we escape into our lab, he turns me to him. "How would you like some free time?"

"What, how? I don't want to put anyone in danger."

"Don't worry about it. No one'll be in danger."

The dear lady from the staff who'd been so kind to me at the beginning of this enters the lab. "I told you things would be all right, Cherie. This card will only have life for another twenty-four hours. After that, it'll be useless." She hands me a security card and gives me a hug. The hug reminds me of the last one I had, with Mom.

My eyes are watery when I look back at her. "Thank you!"

She leaves just as quietly as she'd approached. I look at Al in awe. How did he know I needed this? As he hugs me, for the first time I feel those butterflies in my stomach people talk about. Then he moves in and I think he might kiss me. The only memory I have of a kiss was at a party with Science Olympiads. Someone had decided it would be fun to play spin the beaker. When a spin had landed on me, I was completely surprised and full of dread. I'd not wanted my first kiss to be this way. When we'd leaned in from the circle and our mouths almost touched, the boy actually burped. Gross! I find myself now still apprehensive even though I'm older than I was back then.

I look forward to kissing Al, just not right now. I grasp Al in a tighter hug instead. At first, it's awkward like maybe he had not planned on kissing me, but when I feel the muscles on his back move when he grips me back, the butterflies return. I don't really want to let go of him, but the urge to look at the security card overrides my reverie.

The name on the card breaks my entrancement. This is one of Rigled's old cards. I bet I can access anywhere with this! I quickly hide it in my lab coat pocket, not wanting anyone to discover this treasure. I look back at Al with the biggest smile I've had since leaving Mom. I know what my first venture with this key will be.

When we're escorted to our incubators that night, Colsam seems depressed.

"I'm sorry about Rigled, Colsam." I place a hand on his right arm while behind him on the railcar.

"You have nothing to be sorry for. You're not the one in charge." He hovers his left hand over my right one. He doesn't touch me but there's an electric buzz. Then he clears his throat and replaces his hand to driving position. I leave my hand on his arm just a second longer before pulling it back. I gulp air before I speak.

"I know, but I think it might be kind of my fault. I stood between Rigled and the vulture so he couldn't attack."

"So I've heard." A half-smile breaks through his sad face. "Wish I could've seen that, but don't blame yourself, Vienna. Cromwell's always looking for a reason to torture."

"What do you mean?"

"I think losing his family broke him."

"Oh." I don't know how to respond.

We approach my place.

"Night, Vienna," Colsam chokes out, as if the life were drained from him.

"We'll find a way to change things," I promise him. I want to place my hand back on his arm but decide against it. I need to focus.

I prepare for my journey like a well-travelled camper not wasting any time apart from my hands shaking. When lights begin to turn off, I remove the foldable tablet from the dresser. Since I was forced to hack the system here while working with Charlie, I'm comfortable traipsing into the database now.

After twenty minutes of deciphering and also encrypting my work, I figure out how to open my incubator door. Once it's open and I have access to the screen outside, I'm able to move the railcar. F-R-E-E-D-O-M!!! I sigh in relief but really, I haven't moved an inch and it's taken me almost a half of a flipping hour. As the car pulls up to my location, I hop on board and insert Rigled's card. Now I have free access to travel, as I like. Guess Cromwell wasn't planning on this card providing transportation after the fight.

I cringe with every creak of the railcar. Somehow, I make the successful journey to the other cliff, feeling as though I'd crossed a finish line but at a loss for what to do when I approach Dad's chambers. His lights are off, but I hear movement within. This is the closest I've been to him thus far on the trip, hell in the past decade. I breathe in and rub my hands, but they won't stop shaking. When I enter the algorithm at the podium (thankful each is well placed on the back of Rigled's security card), the screen turns green, and his door opens. My heart skips a beat. I enter his incubator with the excitement of a seven-year-old.

He looks up startled but quickly smiles. He extends his arms to me and tears threaten to spill. I've dreamt about this moment so many times. I close the gap between us as quickly as I can. Hugging my dad after all these years, it feels like a boulder has been lifted from on top of my heart. As we embrace, old family memories fly through my head in a slideshow.

"Sierra, honey, how'd you get here?" He pushes away to get a better look at my face.

I pull out Rigled's card and show him. I notice my hands are still shaking. I hope he'll pull me back into a hug.

"I'm surprised that still works," he says as he stares at the card.

"Only for the next day." Uh, the boulder threatens to drop back on my heart. How am I going to see him again after this? Now I'm the one clearing my throat as Colsam had.

He places his hands on my shoulders, looking at me as if he's double-checking that I'm real. "Ah, it's so good to see you. You've grown up. Last time I saw you, I could still carry you. Now you're a beautiful young lady."

I should pinch myself to make sure this is real. My dad's okay. He remembers me. He remembers US! "You look the same, Dad, well, except for your hair." How do you pick up conversation with someone you haven't seen in so long? It should be easy, right.

"Yeah, I let it grow out. Your Mom would never approve. How is she?"

Great, she's great, even throwing away all of your multidimensional prism photos she's so good. "She's good, still a psychologist. She misses you." This is an awkward sandwich with two slices of awkward and I'm in the middle.

He drops his head and runs his fingers through his hair. I look around his place and flashbacks of experiences with him I'd forgotten return. I distinctively remember being on top of his shoulders as a child, feeling taller than the world around me. I notice he's scooted his dresser closer to the glass bubble and on top of it are milk cartons, plastic spoons, and straws. I also see pieces of fabric from old clothes. I take a step closer to it.

"Dad, are you making cheese?"

He chuckles. "Yeah."

Always experimenting. I notice some small bottles of acetic acid and alcohol, test tubes, and a thermometer. He must have taken these from the lab. Maybe I can save this moment by focusing on our longtime friend and companion, studies.

"What are you doing with this?" I ask as I lift one of the bottles.

"Oh, just isolating casein from the milk."

"Really?"

"Yeah, want to test it out?" He smiles as he hands me a pair of latex gloves.

It is so good to be working on a study with him again. Though as a kid we mostly did things like baking soda and vinegar volcanoes. It's as if we haven't missed a beat. I take a carton of casein curds and scoop a few into one of the test tubes using a spoon. There it is, that look, the one I remember. He's in deep study now. A tornado could come through here and he wouldn't know. Dad grabs a bottle from his lavatory. "I concocted Biuret Reagent."

"How'd you do that?"

He shakes his head looking at the floor. "I've been here for so long."

"Yeah, you have." I take the bottle and pour the reagent into the test tube. As it turns violet, I see the twinkle in my dad's hazel eyes that I've yearned to see for years.

"You did it, Dad!"

"Looks like I did. What about you, baby? It seems you've been fairly successful in life. How in the world did you get to Planet Vortex at only age sixteen?"

"Well, they think I'm nineteen. I faked a laboratory specialist ID using your old identification cards and I go by the name of Vienna."

"What about school, Sierra?"

Seriously, after all of this time it's like he never left. "Dad!" I roll my eyes. Then I remember the other question I have. "Hey, do I have a brother?"

"Yes, honey, you do or maybe you did. I don't know," he says with the placid, non-smiling look Mom's worn over the last almost decade.

"What do you mean maybe I did?" I want to scream.

"Your mom was pregnant when I was taken."

"Um, I'm pretty sure even at six I'd remember that."

"No, sweetheart, you wouldn't because the World Government extracted the embryo and moved it to a lab placenta."

"What? Why would they do that?"

"Because she was a single parent."

"And a damn good one. I thought a parent had to be proven as incapable of raising a child before a child was removed."

"There's a lot about the World Government that you don't know."

"Uh! Wait, but how did you know?"

"One of the doctors brought here shortly after me had been the one to perform the procedure."

"Dad, that's awful. I want to find my brother."

"I know you do but it's impossible. Trust me, I've tried."

He hugs me then.

"As much as I love seeing you, I wish you hadn't come here. You have to get out before something bad happens to you."

"I only came here to bring you back home. We can leave as soon as I find a way to escape."

He grabs my hand, "Um, about that." My insides begin to twist as I see the look of angst on his face. It's the look he had when he told me about Grandma passing away.

My eyes search the desert outside his incubator to avoid his heart-wrenching stare. Between the crater-filled hills, I spy the once frightening vultures now playing together in a game of chase and am deeply jealous of their closeness. My incubator is solitary confinement. Though I'm now standing in my father's quarters, I still feel alone. In my hopeful quest to rescue him, I'd never considered his reaction. I simply skirted over the thought and focused on strategic planning, missing the hunter behind the camouflage veil.

"I can't go," he continues, crushing every bit of strength I had remaining.

"What? Why?" I just got him back and yet he plans to separate us again.

"Follow the map. I believe Colsam can hide you on a shuttle," he says to me while removing a handwritten map from his dresser. "There should be another shuttle in sixteen days."

"But I came here to bring you home," I counter. "Wouldn't the government let you and Mom have my brother back if you were together again?"

"I know, honey, and it means the world to me to be able to see you again, but I have to stop the activity here. I don't believe the World Government will ever return him. And, someone must step up to Cromwell. As his right-hand man, the responsibility is mine. I gave him much of the intelligence he's using now, you see. I wish I could go with you, but I can't. I have to be sure everyone's safe. You can continue my studies. That's the only real thing I've ever stood for."

"But what about Mom? She's missed you all these years. What about me? I want my dad back!"

"I'll be present through your studies. Trust me, I want to be there, but if I left people here to Cromwell's devices, I wouldn't really return to Earth. Part of my soul would forever reside here. It would implode my heart."

"But, Dad, I can't...I need you."

"Oh, sweetie, you're so much tougher than I'll ever be."

He embraces me again and I don't want to lose the comfort it brings.

The moons have shifted, and I know it's getting late. Dad looks at the moons too.

"Better get back to your quarters before you're found out, honey. I truly reside in your heart. That's where I've been for the past years. You make me so proud. It's not a matter of where my body will be, but of where my heart will be. It will be with you always. That little voice you hear will be me guiding you forward. I love you, Sierra."

"I love you too, Dad." I regretfully leave his quarters to return to mine. He gave me the answers I yearned for, how to escape this place. However, if it's without him, I won't escape. Part of me will be stuck here forever too. I don't know why I thought I could just come here and rescue him. If a tornado can't pull him away from his studies, how can I?

10

BREAK

Vienna

AT BREAKFAST, THINGS ARE AWKWARD, AND I NOTICE Yesha doesn't say a thing. She's sitting with our group but she's not saying a word and keeps darting her eyes around the room. So, I sit next to her and whisper. "Yesha, what were you doing in an off-limits section? Why didn't you let me know that you gained access?"

"You wouldn't even be here if it wasn't for me. No need to get miffed."

I'm so caught off guard that I don't respond at first. "Hey, just trying to figure out what's going on…you know, for my purpose here." I look around to double check no one's listening.

"Uh, I guess I have to tell you then. The reason I didn't want to come here is because I lost someone very close to me from this place. Since I'm here, I might as well make it worth it."

So apparently, I'm not the only one here with an alternate cause, though hers seems more of a vendetta. Who did she lose? Why didn't she ask for my help? Was I so focused on my dad that I completely ignored Yesha?

Right then Dr. Cromwell approaches our table, "Vienna, I saw in the readings how you escaped possible intrusion into a non-bio study by hiding some findings. Most would be reluctant to do so, but you saw that it could act as a placebo. Bravo!"

"Thank you!" I think that's what I should say here, but find it difficult to say it to this man. I never fathomed ever holding a conversation with him and is he really complimenting me for breaking the rules? "I just acted out of gut response, though."

"Well, your gut's right on. I'd like you to accompany me through a couple of procedures."

I don't miss the looks from everyone at the table, but can't let go of the opportunity, scary as it may be. Perhaps Colsam had been right about keeping your enemies closer. I haven't been able to learn how to successfully convince my dad, so maybe befriending the enemy will get me there.

"Follow me. I've something to show you."

I mimic his moves and try to avoid the looks of disbelief directed our way. He opens a dark green door with a retina scan. The same holographic screens I'd seen with Yesha depict our moves as we walk down a hallway. I feel as though I could be walking death row, but I also have a reassuring sense that this is a required move for my objective.

He must see my look of fright, "No, no! I'm not going to harm you. In fact, you remind me of what my child would be like had he lived. I just want to run a few tests. Don't worry, I'm going to take every precaution."

I have a whirlwind of thoughts. I can't trust this man. What kind of tests does he want to run and why? The way he's talking to me is different from how I've seen him in the facility before. Then he departs to collect what he needs for the study. Part of me wants to escape now, but the urge to stay and find a way to free Dad is too strong.

I look around to see if there's anything I can use as a weapon if Cromwell's true intentions aren't good ones. I see framed multidimensional prism photographs of his wife and child everywhere. One is a picture of all three of them. I walk over to it. Cromwell's looking at his wife, smiling. For a second he looks like a caring person. At the bottom of the multidimensional prism photo, it reads "Henry, Sorna, and Damien Cromwell." Sorna looks too kind and Damien looks like a regular kid. He has a mischievous grin as if he's about to break a rule.

I hear his footsteps and return to my seat.

"I see that you are like me. You want to conduct scientific research, without interruption," Cromwell says as he opens a metal suitcase full of electrodes, vials, and needles.

"Vienna, I'm interested in knowing your intelligence level. I'm going to place a few probes and ask you some questions. This is just a simple scientific study." This isn't what I expected. I guess an intelligence test is pretty harmless.

"Okay, may I see the results too?" I ask. I don't like him getting this close to me, but if I want to get close to him, I guess it's necessary.

"Of course, I'm delighted to hear of your interest," he says as he faces a screen my direction. This holograph has a protector on the backside so that information cannot be seen unless you are on the front side. "I'll be running a Brain Performance Index test alongside an Electroencephalogram. Okay, that's the last probe. Are you ready?"

"Yeah." How gross. The evil madman's hands actually touched me. I found some comfort when he put on gloves but find myself hurting a little. He must not want to be too close to me. I know that shouldn't bother me, but it feels like picking at a blister that's been there a very long time.

He pulls another screen up next to the test screen to record results. The first question shows a list of numbers and asks which one doesn't belong. These are usually primes or algebraic formulas, but this one is of square roots.

"Twenty-eight."

He taps the screen for the next question. I find myself excited to see what it is, even though I'm still trembling inside. The question depicts four diagrams and asks which of the following four would be the next in sequence. Good thing I enjoyed digital Origami as a child. I fold the paper in my head.

"D."

He taps the screen again. The letters displayed are RLAY and asks if they stand for a planet, a moon, a constellation, or a solar system.

"Constellation."

I actually find myself enjoying the test, eager to see the results. Perhaps I'm just as much of a madman as Cromwell himself. No, I would never cross the lines he has to abuse others. In my life, I've found some lines to be a bit fuzzy and easy to go back and forth on, but when it comes to activities that knowingly cause harm, I believe the lines are very firm. Look at Dad, even suffering years in this place, he's compelled to continue to save others where he can. That's when my enjoyment ends. Cromwell looks disheartened at the results.

"Um, Vienna, I don't mean to pry, but at what point in your cycle are you?"

I drop my jaw in disbelief.

"No, no, it's nothing like that. Studies on the female brain show differential in IQ at different points in the cycle. For two weeks, a female brain surgeon will test higher than her male counterparts will. During the other two weeks, she'll test equal to or slightly lower than they will. This would be useful knowledge for you to have too. You can schedule important things during the hormonal shift of the higher two weeks."

While this all makes sense, I guess, I still hesitate like a five-year-old jumping off the diving board for the first time. I don't want him to know that much about me. I did just peek at his family multidimensional prism photos though. "I'm on day twenty-five."

"Ah, that explains a lot. I would like to run these tests again in about two weeks. I was going to run some labs, but I think it best to wait until then."

Good, that gives me more time to find his weaknesses and strategize. "Sounds good." What labs though? Worry surfaces like a submarine to use deck guns.

"Do you remember the way out?" he asks.

"Yeah, I can manage." Wait, he never told me the results. Oh, cog it all.

———

I walk to my lab full of questions. What if Cromwell won't open up to me until my score is higher? How am I going to free my dad when he's determined to stay? When I walk into the lab and a latex glove flies my way, I'm actually able to smile. We don't have an attending physician here today. We can be free for just a little while. I grab a box of gloves and hide behind one of the tables.

Viscerous makes a move to get an angle on me but Albina snaps him in the side with a glove. He sits down, muttering behind a smile. I catch Al moving to the stairs that lead to where attending physicians usually stand. I see my chance and move to the faucet. As I hide behind the sink, I see Al slap Albina with a glove. She saunters over to Viscerous and sits with him, whispering. I reach my hands above the sink and fill a glove with water.

"Hey, that's against the rules," Al shouts as he begins to climb the stairs.

I catch him in the back with the makeshift water balloon. When he turns around with eyes as big as silver dollars, I roll on the floor laughing!

"That's it," Al says now above me on the other side of the sink. When the water turns on, I look up. He has a bucket. As I shuffle and scurry along the floor using beds and cabinets as my shield, I see Viscerous and Albina pointing and laughing. As I turn the corner, I see boots. When the bucket begins to spill, I stand up, turning it the opposite way. Al and I are soaked, but we're both laughing. He pulls me into him and my breath catches.

"You started it," he says moving drenched hair out of my face.

"Hey, I just walked in here and a glove was thrown my way. My intelligence just outweighed yours."

"Is that what he was doing with you? Testing your intelligence?" Al asks without the humor he had before. He steps back.

"Maybe, what's it to you?"

Al's face crumples with my response. "Be careful, Vienna. We just witnessed the results of brain matter transplantation before you left," Viscerous chimes in.

"Don't worry. I have a reason to get close to Cromwell," I respond. Too late, I realize that I've said too much.

"What's your reason, darling?" Albina asks for the group.

They're all looking at me in expectation. I didn't want to put them in harm's way. I've held this in for so long that it doesn't come easily. I open my mouth to say something and then close it. I take a breath in and then exhale the words quickly before I can change my mind.

"Septimus is my dad. I want to save him. Well, that was

my initial motive. Now, after witnessing life here, I no longer think that's enough."

They all nod and clasp fisted hands, and I find myself in their center. "What do you think we've been doing here? Twiddling our thumbs in the midst of chaos?" Al asks me.

Albina goes to a cabinet and begins pulling out handwritten maps and notes.

"We've been trying to find a way to escape for some time now," Viscerous says.

They have the schedule for the guards, a map of the entire medical facility including a five-mile radius, and they have Cromwell's schedule. "How did you locate Cromwell's schedule? I would have thought it would have been sealed shut away from anyone."

"Many people in power adhere to strict schedules," Al says. "Remember the woman who brought you Rigled's card, Cora? She is also Cromwell's secretary, and she hates what's being done here. She lost her only daughter to one of the experiments. Do you think she stays here out of loyalty?"

"So, was the map derived from your experiences and off-facility trips?" I ask before taking a breath, thinking of the kind woman who gave me Rigled's security card.

"Partially, but we also have ties to the population outside this facility," Albina says.

"How?" I'm asking again.

"Most of the guards didn't volunteer to be here but were forced with charges, sometimes true, mostly false," Viscerous answers.

"So that's how you've come up with their schedules too," I say. "May I ask who your lead communication's been with?"

"Wait no, before we tell you more, what was Septimus' first discovery?" Albina says.

"That's easy. Robotic bloodstream inhibitors that fight viruses," I answer, knowing that this should be classified information. They give me looks of admiration; perhaps my dad has opened up to them more than I realized.

"You really are his daughter," Al says. "Wow, I owe the man my life for saving me." He clasps his fingers around my forearm in a friendly, admiring way. Heat surges up to my shoulder.

"Our lead communication's with a guard by the name of Colsam," Viscerous says. I should have known.

"Where's the population outside of the facility?" I ask. "We didn't see anyone during the water trip."

"Cromwell specifically chose the most isolated part of this planet to build the facility," Albina answers as she points to possible population spots outside the five-mile radius on the map.

"Our biggest obstacle is how to get everyone out," Al says. "It wouldn't feel right leaving others behind."

"I think my dad's been working on something that can help us with that. He's probably been working on it for years. I saw milk in his incubator. I believe he's isolating tryptophan through hydrolysis of casein."

"So that's where you went with the key," Al says.

"A sleeping pill for Cromwell?" Viscerous asks with a mischievous grin much like the one Damien wore in the multidimensional prism photo. "That's marvelous. Maybe it could work."

"Yeah, but we can't fit everyone on a single shuttle," Al says.

"Slipping him a sleeping pill more than once would be impossible," Albina says.

An unsettling realization hits me. "So what *are* you planning?"

"Well," Viscerous looks at the others for approval. "We think a revolt is the best way to get most of us out of here. The number of those willing to fight Cromwell is steadily increasing, but Colsam's been unable to persuade many of the guards. This is their home planet, and Cromwell is tightly knit with the government here. The guards won't fight until they're guaranteed amnesty."

A revolt with most of the guards still on Cromwell's side would lead to bloodshed. "I think if I'm able to get closer to Cromwell, I could help the process without risking lives like a revolution would."

"No!" Al almost yells. "He's done enough damage. It's time to fight."

He squeezes my forearm, and I feel as if I'm being torn in two. I care for him, but my drive to save Dad is stronger. "Al, you could lose those you care about in a coup. Anything can happen here. Nothing's a given. I have to help."

He just walks off and begins the necessary studies so Cromwell will think we've been following instructions. Albina pats my arm and pulls me aside.

"What else did Cromwell say to you?"

"He'll be running tests again in a couple of weeks."

She rolls her eyes before responding. "He holds a lot of power. Don't let his sexist and prejudicial statements bring you down. Stay strong, okay! Don't question yourself around him."

"Okay." Her statements ring true. I need to be sure not to let his beliefs infiltrate my thoughts.

Then, she and Viscerous begin their own studies. Before I turn to do the same, I go to the cabinet Albina had opened. Sure enough, I find the wires and sensors I thought I saw. I take a few and put them in my pocket to store in my quarters. I decide I will figure out a way to stop Cromwell without putting others in harm's way. Al might not believe it's possible, but I'll prove him wrong.

———

I spot two guards heading in my direction as I'm turning the corner of a hallway. I take a step back around the corner and lean against the wall. I can hear them speaking to one another.

"They said I was making illegal bets on Waterbag tournaments. I don't know how they got the charges to stick. I've never made a bet with Kroon in my life."

"That sounds just like my trial. Said I was involved with drugs, but I've never even taken Pycnogenol to relieve pain."

"Were you ever involved in sports?"

"I wasn't betting on them if that's what you're asking."

"No, I mean did you ever compete? I've noticed that many of us labeled as criminals were athletes at one point in our lives."

"Well, yeah, I played back in guidance institute."

"I think they've targeted the athletic types to be guards."

I'm so engaged in their conversation that I almost forget to move from my location before the guards turn the corner. I walk only a few feet before we're in the same hallway. I imagine running down the hall away from them, but my daydream turns into one of them tackling me. I decide against fleeing.

"Where are you headed?" one of the guards asks me.

"I'm going to my lab."

The other guard looks at my identification card and says, "Your lab's that way." He points his finger over my shoulder, the way I just came from, and moves so that each blocks a direction.

The first guard places a hand on his weapon and looks me in the eye. I spot Al in my periphery from an adjoining hallway and notice that instead of the angry glance I would have predicted, he looks concerned for me.

"Guess I was daydreaming and got turned the wrong way. Thank you for correcting me." I'm fearful of the guard's hand. I know what it can do. I reach into the depths of any strength I have left and play the only card I can. I fist my right hand

and hold it over the left side of my chest like some of the guards had after Rigled's brutal death. The other guard drops his jaw. The guard with his hand on his weapon moves his arm and returns the gesture. Then he steps aside and allows me to walk to my lab as I breathe in a sigh of relief. I spy Al turning to walk the same way. I'm glad when the guards turn a corner. The sense of walking on pins and needles doesn't escape until we head to the cafeteria. Spots swim into my vision and I stagger. I have to squeeze my eyes shut and shake my head before I can take a step forward. It seems with my increased meditation abilities my emotions and the emotions of those around me are causing me to be more prone to fainting which is rather annoying.

———

"I found out what happened to my brother," Yesha tells me at lunch.

"What happened to him?" I ask while shifting the succulent juice cans around in my pockets. I'm going to attempt sneaking these into my quarters too.

"He was supposed to swap arteries with Viscerous."

A couple of seats down Viscerous holds up his hands, lowering his head in a sign of surrender.

"Septimus tried to save him. If Cromwell would've listened to him, my brother would still be alive. I think we should kill Cromwell so Septimus can lead here. He'd be much better at it."

"Possibly, but does the facility even need to exist?" I ask, disturbed by the thought of my dad leading here for the rest of his life. In eleven days, Cromwell will test me again. In exactly the same number of days, a shuttle will be on Planet Vortex that could take my dad away from this place. I need to move faster than I have been.

"Think of the wonders, the scientific findings this place would produce in his hands," an awestruck Yesha exclaims.

"Many of the guards are loyal to Cromwell," I point out. "I don't think an assassination is the answer."

A hush falls over everyone, and they all look above my head. I turn around to see what's caught everyone's interest.

"Vienna, Cromwell needs your help with a procedure this afternoon," the flame-throwing guard says approaching the table. "Could you please follow me?" What in the world? It hasn't been two weeks.

Al shoves his tray away when I rise. My insides feel like a drone bug that's lost its power, spiraling out of control.

As we exit the cafeteria, we meet Cromwell just outside the door and the guard walks off to another task. "What procedure are we working on today?" I ask Cromwell.

"Limb transplant." He doesn't miss my look of distaste at his answer. "I know you prefer the use of non-bio bodies over live hosts, but I just don't have a choice. Many non-bio bodies we've studied have shown symptoms of deflection. Even if seventy percent of non-bio bodies show no signs of alteration, I can't settle for less than perfection."

"Why is perfection necessary? Why can't we continue study and improve processes on non-bio bodies? What about cloning?"

"No, I accept nothing less than perfection. Human clones can only copy the current state of the subject so they're not ideal in many accident or illness situations."

All I can do is contract my muscles, so I'm able to gulp through my wool-encased throat. I hope for a change of mood, but instead it continues to decline.

"I met Sorna in a park. Never in a million years did I imagine I'd find someone else like me, full of intellect and way beyond run of the mill. When we united and produced a child of our own, which we named Damien, we were both surprised at the love we had for him. We could only imagine what kind of genius had been formed. When Sorna and Damien were taken from me, I snapped. Vultures assaulted them with beak plunges through their bodies. I found a greater reason for my studies. I'll never be satisfied so long as Sorna and Damien are gone."

I can't believe he shared so much with me. Part of me wishes he hadn't. Now I understand just how driven he really is, but maybe I can use his openness to get closer to him. I want to ask why the vultures attacked. They seem like friendly enough creatures. I don't want to push him away with questions like that.

"I'm sorry about your family," I say.

"I should have made clones of them before that ever happened. Making clones after they're dead would only clone them in that state...dead. Also, the storage of clones before they're ready to be activated has proven to be problematic. Even cloning them before the accident would not have worked. I would have had to confine the clones and the experience would have changed their nurtured personalities."

"We'll find a way to revive them." Another lie. I don't how he thinks he can save them from the dead. It's got to be too late now.

He smiles down at me.

My insides feel like they've been dipped in glue. I do have something in common with this man. Don't I ignore others' needs in my attempts to rescue Dad? I'm in utter turmoil, as though I'm losing my mind as much as Cromwell himself. At least I've found his Achilles' heel.

11
TIME WARP

Al

CROMWELL MIGHT BE PRECISION BUT CROMWELL AND Septimus together is far superb. Septimus is the engineer and the artist of procedures, placing each piece where it should be while Cromwell is the vision, contemplating things no one else sees and making the chess moves no one expects. But today something seems off.

"In this study we were able to locate the closest genomic match but, without an update, there's still 20% chance of error," Septimus tells Cromwell as he points to the holograph screen.

"Why?" Cromwell rubs his forehead.

When they're together I'm able to see what Cromwell once was. It's as if they're lifelong chums and the studies take them back to their University days.

"Genomic mutation…" Septimus begins but is interrupted by Cromwell shoving a chair.

"Time's running out!" Cromwell says.

"I get it," Septimus replies but Cromwell gives him a nod before looking down and rubbing his fingers from temple to nose as if swiping tears.

Is Cromwell crying?

"We'll just have to gather more samples," Cromwell says.

"But, that's…" Septimus is unable to finish as Cromwell exits.

If only I could continue watching Septimus who's turned back to the studies, but Cromwell's moving fast.

What was he talking about, gathering more samples?

———

Being in the tunnels reminds me of the home. They had tunnels too. And, just like now, I use them to get an advantage to save the abused. I wonder what it will take to get Septimus to partner with the revolution. Maybe I can circle back and see him more after I've finished following Cromwell.

It's difficult to keep up with Cromwell's quick step.

What's he in such a hurry for?

I'm able to catch up while he's going through a retina scan. In the lab I see her. She's somewhat adjusted to life here, but she needs to be careful. Vienna's against the revolution. She has some school age notion that she can fix things here. She doesn't get it. Things don't change when they're this corrupt. It's too far gone.

"What's that?" Cromwell asks her.

"I've located a hole in the non-bio studies. I've theorized that non-bios could reach the desired purity goal if we close the gap," she says.

"You do have an eye for details and specifics, don't you?"

Cromwell places a hand on her shoulder, and they make

eye contact. Is that a blush? Vienna's cheeks are pink when she turns back to the study.

What the hell! It's too late when I realize I've punched the tunnel wall.

"Damn it, I'm going to have inspect the tunnels for rodents again," Cromwell says.

"I'm sure it was just dust moving in there. I've noticed an increase in sand within the facility."

"You have? We'll have to vacuum them out then."

Now she puts a hand on his shoulder to turn his attention back to the study. I could swear she looks directly at me before shaking her head back and forth.

"Well, I think I've improved the live host acceptance using genetic mutation."

"Really, how's that?"

She waves her hand behind her back indicating that I should leave.

I don't want to but it's probably for the best. I make a mental note to sit Vienna down for a discussion soon. I'm expected elsewhere anyway.

———

Colsam found a new place for us to meet. There's a blind spot in one of the hallway alcoves AND the only microphone within reach is down. I can count the number of times I've been able to speak freely outside of the lab but within the confines of the facility on one hand.

"Took you long enough, Sweetheart. What, were you painting your nails?"

I punch him in the arm in response. I guess if Viscerous and Albina are my pseudo parents, Colsam's like my brother.

"Yeah right. I was in the tunnels, jerk face."

"Dude, you have to be careful up there! You know you're going to get caught one of these days."

"I know. Cromwell even heard me today."

Colsam gives me a nudge, pushing my shoulders back.

"I freaking told you." He rolls his eyes at me in disapproval.

"You should have seen the way he touched Vienna."

"He what?" Colsam begins to yell but restrains himself.

"Hey, it's not that big of a deal all right. What's it to you anyway?"

He clears his throat as I rub away a scuff mark on the floor with my boot.

"So, anyway, how many guards do we have now?"

"We're about 25%."

"Shit, that's not enough."

"I know. Theopat's trying to get more government pull."

"Hey, be careful. You think my crawling in tunnels is bad? It's got nothing on messing with the government. I hate the jerks."

"Relax, man."

"What about weapons?"

"That we have plenty of. Thanks for the idea of amping up the Airblow. Great work."

I nod and he laughs.

Another guard walks by. One that's not on our side yet. I recognize him as one of the guards who had been celebrating with Cromwell.

"Get back to your lab," Colsam commands me.

"Is this employee failing to follow our guidelines, Colsam?"

"No, no, he was just leaving. Thanks though."

I walk away but the guard continues to stare me down. I hear him as I turn the corner.

"You can't let them get away with stuff like that! You losing your nerve or what? You've been acting weird lately," the guard says to Colsam.

Crap! I really hope he's not busted. What would we do then?

12
ROAD TRIP

Vienna

WITHIN A LABORATORY I'VE NEVER BEEN TO BEFORE appears two dangling arms submerged in an icy bath. What once were perfectly functioning extremities now weave like virtual reality algae in a wave. As Dr. Cromwell appears behind me, breathing down my neck, I know I must appear captivated by the scene in order to gain his trust. It's hard to be fascinated when bile rises up my esophagus.

The laboratory is behind one of the restricted doors. Cromwell had to perform a retina scan for entry. Technology here is more like home than what we have in my lab. The robotic lab technician gives instructions and is ready to step in if a doctor is unable to perform. The technician reminds me of my clopil at home, Vex, except with a more human form and pearlish color. The doctors are some of the ones that I've never seen before. I wonder if they normally work beside my dad.

For his experiment today, Cromwell took two healthy

human beings and removed an arm from each of them. He instructs me to grab one of the arms as another laboratory specialist grabs the other. Doing this feels as if I'm dipping my hand into a sea of dead bodies. Next, I'm to connect the arm to the other body. I use a protoplasm suture machine to stitch every nerve, artery, and vein ending with the perfection of an Olympic athlete. Luckily, Dad taught me to suture when I was young. We'd been on a hiking trip and he cut his back. The cut was so deep I could see his muscle exposed. I was quite young, but he couldn't reach the cut.

Right now, I'm void of the comfort of Dad's knowledge though. It's vile participating in one of Cromwell's experiments. When the patients are awake from anesthesia, I insert stem cells to initiate their bodies' acceptance of a foreign object. I mistakenly look into one of the subject's eyes. The eerie and defeated look is what I kind of imagine I'd see at the sentencing of an innocent murder trial defendant. I try to swallow my disgust as Dr. Cromwell reviews my sutures.

"Job well done. Your hands are steady," Cromwell encourages me.

"Will they move now like a natural arm?" I ask him.

"Not at first, but in time. The tissue will soon adapt like natural movement, involuntarily."

"How many times have you seen organic movement be successful?"

"The odds outweigh non-bio three to one."

"And that's why you need live hosts?" I ask the question I'd been pondering but wonder how much of a wack job he must be to think he can bring Sorna and Damien back from the dead.

"Of course—you're catching on quickly."

When I return to my incubator that night, I feel as though important parts of me have become numb. I toss and turn. I miss Mom and wish she was here to discuss these things with.

At least there are others on my side, but the thought of those I've become close to putting themselves in danger makes my rib cage ache. As though an elephant's been stepping on my torso. Some of these aches will never go away, even if I free everyone here.

I need to fall asleep. Time's closing in on me, as in the days of cramming for finals. All I can picture are limbs swimming in an icy bath; part of me wants to call it embalming liquid as the extremity has lost the life it once knew.

When I look across to my dad's incubator, I see the same sign language. Instead of just repeating the symbol back, I urge more communication. I sign asking if he knows about Cromwell trying to save his family, and my dad answers back with, *what?* I realize he can't see me properly, so I pull out the tablet and begin investigating. I'm shocked when I find what I'm looking for, instructions to the frosted glass. I notice that there aren't hammock building instructions. Once I find the switch and have turned off the glass, I look to see if video magnification is available on the tablet. When I find that it is, I almost feel as if this must be a trap. But I still can't hold myself back from communicating with Dad. I signal directions for him to remove the frost and use a magnifier too.

Have you been working with Cromwell to try to save his wife and kid?

We're not playing children's games here, Sierra. You need to keep your distance.

But it's the reason he's keeping you here, isn't it?

His hands raise in a halting position and then he continues.

I've pushed to stay because I need to help those in danger. I don't want you to become one of them.

But why? Away from us? There has to be another way.

There still are true scientific findings happening here. Plus, I can't put you and your mom at risk. It's why I left in the first place. He threatened you. Looks like that didn't work out the way I planned.

My dad wasn't just kidnapped but extorted. With his departure, he could save Mom and me. It would be wonderful if I could travel back to before that time, when one of my biggest worries was if Mom would let me have ice cream after dinner. I just want to be able to enjoy time with Dad. I'm tired of worrying about everything at the facility.

Dad, what was my favorite bedtime story when I was seven before you were taken? I ask, and my pajamas flutter with the shaking of my body.

Talented Tillie, of course. You had me read you that days on end. I was so grateful when the author, Randi Hacker, signed a copy for you.

He does remember. This is my dad. The years here have eroded him away like a brick building in centuries of rain, but the foundation stands. With this finding, tiredness has finally weighed in. I sign "I love you" to him one more time, and when he signs back, I shut off the light.

Even though I'm tired, I'm unable to fall asleep because of all the things still bouncing in my head. I use the tablet to program the sensors I took from the lab and then use it to open the door again. I grab the wires and sensors from the lab, the juice cans from the cafeteria, and break out the glass from the handheld mirror in the lavatory. I had noticed part of the wall covered by incubator rock when we went on the water expedition. At all times of the day, it's kept from view. Guards don't see it. No one can see it unless they have just the right angle and know what they're looking for.

I head in that direction being as quiet as I can and keeping a lookout for the sign of any guards. Once there, I begin construction. Using the surrounding rocks for support, I line the cans with the glass so that it can receive the only ray of moon and sun light to reach this place. I'll be able to remote

3-D print from the tablet. It will use the sand around it for material. I'll have to revisit to move sand closer, but I should be able to build a ladder over the wall. Then, if there's enough time, I can find more tools and material and build shuttles. I'll have to find more tech-savvy equipment than I have for the ladder to even come close to meeting my deadline, but it gives me hope.

———

In my lab the next day, all eyes are fixed on me as I tell my companions about the limb transplant.

"Asshole!" Al says looking at his limbs.

I wonder if I should remind Al about Cromwell's preference for live over bionic testing but decide against it. It really doesn't make sense. Just looking at Al…he's perfection right in front of me.

"Forget him, Al," Viscerous says. "Now's not the time. We're not ready."

"We should act on Yesha's theory," Al says. "I do have the Airblow! Or we could give him too much sleeping pill."

I find myself grabbing his forearm as he had me except my move feels like more than friendship. My insides feel as if they're being mixed in a cauldron. I imagine Al using the Airblow against the guards, outnumbered and falling quickly. What is this aspired brew? This is not the direction I wanted to go.

An announcement by Cromwell sounds over the intercom. "Facility members, we're in need of more stem cells. The factory line's a half-mile away. A guard will come around to collect those who've been assigned to this task. Everyone else is to maintain their schedules."

We all look at each other in surprise.

"Been awhile since we've had to do this," Viscerous says.

"What's the stem cell factory line?" I ask.

"It really should be called a harvesting center," Albina says while rolling her eyes. "I don't know why he calls it a factory."

"There will be tons of apheresis catheters," Al says. "The ones assigned have probably been secretly given medication via cafeteria food or oxygen pills. I haven't been able to pinpoint which, in order to improve stem cell formation and disbursement. My theory's that the medication is in the oxygen pill, and the food has calcium enrichment to counter the depletion of harvesting."

"Will the assigned people have stem cells removed?" I ask. "How do they direct the pills and food to only those people?"

"The systems in place here are very sophisticated," Albina says.

"And yes, those assigned will have stem cells harvested," Viscerous adds.

Here's something else the people here have had to experience. When does it end? Perhaps the idea of my dad taking over's not as horrible as I thought. Could this place turn into a peaceful laboratory? Could my mom and I live here with Dad? No, I bet Cromwell's thought of this before. His ties to the government would circumvent such a move. My dad would probably be accused of treason and punished. If only the punishment could be extradition to another planet, specifically Earth.

Colsam enters our lab. I haven't had a real conversation with him since the one right after Rigled was killed, but I have been privy to his activities helping those here attempting escape.

"Hi, Colsam," I say as if to a friend, which feels right.

"Hey, Vienna," he says, but not in his usual caring way. His jaw muscles keep tensing, relaxing and then tensing again.

"What's wrong, man?" Viscerous asks him.

"I've been sent to collect three of you and escort you to the stem cell factory."

We all look at each other. It's so quiet the adjustment of a microscope could be heard.

"Which of us are you taking?" Al asks as he squeezes my forearm in a protective manner.

I bet certain people would be chosen as stem cell providers because they have the most viable stem cells.

"You, Viscerous, and Vienna," Colsam's breath catches part way through my name as if there was an "H" between the "I" and the "E." His jaw tightens again.

"No. How can we keep her out of this?" Al asks.

"She should be safe," Albina tries to soothe Al.

Al walks away from me and punches a table, the clang sounding different than if it were from a fist of human flesh.

"I'm sorry, but orders are orders, and if you want to avoid punishment, you'll follow me," Colsam replies.

Viscerous nods, kisses Albina on her forehead, and walks Colsam's way. Al puts an arm around my shoulders as if he can protect me from what I'm about to go through and we join them. Albina waves goodbye as we exit the lab.

We enter the shuttle's airlock like room and Colsam hands us suits and pouches. We prepare for our journey, and it's as if we're the first people to land on the moon. Everyone's jittery and unsure of their next move.

"How long will it take to get to the factory?" I ask Colsam.

"It usually takes minutes, but when I've run across weather or hover malfunction, it's taken me up to an hour so be prepared."

"I'm game for hover malfunction," Al says.

"Good," I smile at them all as I metaphorically twist the latch.

All three men give me a look of amusement as they follow me out into the sauna.

"Ah hey, I need to relieve myself," I say as we approach the hover-bike. They stay behind the bike as I go to the front. I take my pack straw and suck some water in but don't swallow. I scoop a handful of sand and spit water into it. As I cake the now sandy mud onto a rotor, I watch the sun bake the mud into a plaster and begin to harden. We're only going to make it four hundred meters before the rotor stops. I will finally have some time free out in the open. I'll be able to fix the rotor and get us to the factory line afterward, but not before we catch a breath on the beach-like sand.

"Okay, I'm ready to go. Thanks for waiting."

"No problem," Colsam coughs out, laughing at my cover of needing to relieve myself.

Al looks at me, then at the rotor, and then at me again with a sideways smile.

"Pretty impressive with the lack of toilet paper," Viscerous says. "Maybe you could teach Albina how to do that in a suit!"

We all board, Al and I sharing a seat. When his body touches mine, it's like an ocean wave crashing into me, sending my body into a drop, twist, and then rise with the ferocious-ness of a hurricane. Colsam begins driving but soon enough a rotor sputters and we park on the ground. As he steps off the bike to examine it, a vulture drops down next to us. Colsam doesn't jump in fear or engage a weapon. As the vulture walks up to me and drops its head, I recognize it as the one who saved me. After I pet it for a bit, it moves on and approaches Colsam. I cringe in fear, but a game ensues. As Colsam tries to grab one of the vulture's legs, it jumps back and then approaches again. Colsam makes a move for the other leg and the vulture spins.

"Do vultures not dislike you, like the other guards?" I ask Colsam.

"I wasn't the most popular kid. The vultures have been my friends for a long time."

I look at Al and Viscerous to see how they feel about the

creature, but they distance themselves from it, still afraid. I walk up and begin petting the bird again. I've felt so beaten down from this place that the vulture's companionship is a relief. When it drops its head to my feet again, I decide to take a chance. I put one leg over the vulture and grab around its neck. When the vulture lifts off, I think I hear yelling from Al, but quickly forget about it when I'm soaring through the sky. As if the wind can strip away the awful things I have witnessed here.

The vulture flies me around in a circle, giving me the play my lost childhood has thirsted for. We dip behind a cliff, then rise up higher, and I'm in the middle of clouds. The fog hits me like glitter thrown in the air. The vulture then brings me back and allows me to deboard next to Al, who makes sure he stays well beyond beak-plunge distance. Without the magnetic pull from surrounding buildings, I'm stronger here. As if my muscles are having to do less work. And yet, I'm weaker at the same time too.

"Thank you, my Aviator." I pet the bird before it turns and flies away. "Why can't we all just fly off on vultures?" I ask Colsam.

"Because they have inserted microchips," Colsam says. "The second they left their assigned area the government would be on us. They protect the facility, but Cromwell doesn't like them too close. They can approach the quarters area but no closer and cannot leave the perimeter either."

"Well, that's a pity," I say as I remember the feeling of love while I rubbed the vulture's head.

"We better get to the factory before we're missed," Viscerous says.

I walk to the rotor, remove my straw, and blast away the mud I'd applied. Al, Colsam, and Viscerous shake their heads as they watch me. Al's the only one smiling. We board and continue our trip.

We hover through high rocky hills, weaving back and forth in the opposite direction of our water collection. I haven't been able to see beyond these hills from the facility. Once we've passed through dense trails, we're in an open expanse again. I'm unable to look around because a tree-like metal skyscraper stands before us, capturing my attention. Instead of bark, it's as if the metal roots spiral upward, intermingling at the top to branch out and form the crown. The metal branches spread out into a flat spider web instead of a body of leaves. Colsam navigates the hover into a tunnel formed by one of the roots at ground level. Once we've reached the trunk, he parks.

Colsam steps off, his hand brushing mine as he goes, and walks to a grand desk in the center of the room. The desk is round with holographic screens on the surface that glow teal and purple. The building's different from our placid medical facility. Colors bounce off every wall, and the windows have multiple shapes with each root bend. Behind the desk is a female version of the guards, same gray muscular body and mallard-shaped head but with more delicate size and features.

"Theopat."

"Colsam."

There's an awkward silence. The way she looks at him bothers me. Unpopular, my ass.

"Did you hear about the water bag tournament? What an upset."

"Sorry, we're kept out of the loop at the medical facility. Who won?"

"The Kosmos upset the Salyuts ten to three! It was so unexpected and exciting to watch. I wish you could've seen it like old times. One of the Kosmos starters was able to ride the bag counter gravity a hundred yards a pass! Oh, Colsam, I really wish you were out here with us still. The charges they brought against you were slanderous."

"Trust me, I wish I was out here too, but the appeal was useless, so I'm stuck and need to adhere to schedule."

Is Colsam's story about being here to be closer to the enemy a cover, or is what he's telling Theopat the true smoke and mirrors?

"Oh, right, time for more stem cells?"

"Yes, indeed. I'm checking in Al, Viscerous, and Vienna today." He motions for us to follow him to the desk.

She taps a holographic screen a few times and then addresses us. "Welcome to Nephilim. Follow me."

"Well, I'll see you in a couple days," Colsam says as he gets back on the hover.

"What do you mean a couple days?" I ask. Al rubs my shoulder. How am I going to build the ladder?

"Yes, it takes days to get the necessary stem cells," Theopat explains. "It would take twice as long without this structure. The altitude allows for faster stem cell harvesting."

I become mute, as I have no response to this. I don't want to be away from Dad, but what's a couple days added to the years?

As Theopat steps away from the desk, we follow her into a small hallway. I notice multiple doors. We walk to the furthest door in the hallway and Theopat presses a button. As the door slides open, I can see the inner workings of this metal tree. Gears and columns are everywhere. Theopat takes a step into the open with nothing beneath her. I step forward to pull her back, afraid she doesn't realize there isn't a floor, but stop when she doesn't fall. She's standing in the air with nothing below her. It's another incubator.

Al grabs my hand as we step into the incubator. This time I definitely think it feels like more than friends. That's when I see the holograph with numbers. Theopat taps the highest number, sixty, and the elevator rises. It feels as though I'm flying but without the vulture beneath me.

13

FALL

Vienna

I'm thankful for the quick transport, as I don't take a breath the entire way. When the incubator stops, and we're able to step on ground I can see, I do take in a deep breath. There are cots lined up against the walls. Many are already inhabited. I'm grateful that Yesha isn't here.

We walk to a few open cots. Luckily, we can be next to each other. I'm not sure I could handle another new environment without my friends. As I sit on my cot, Theopat retrieves a tablet at the end of the bed. She boots it up and sits next to me. Her behavior's different from the guards at the facility. She seems caring, like the school nurse giving me ice in elementary school when I bumped my head in gym.

"Do you mind if I ask you a few questions, Vienna? Protocol for this type of procedure," Theopat says.

Now I feel like Charlie must have when I'd been asking the questions. "No, shoot away," I say.

Theopat ducks her head nervously as if avoiding a firing squad and then smiles, "I forget about the Earth language. You cannot take everything literally." She laughs as she pats my thigh.

We run through the necessary questions and then she surprises me with the last one. "Do you mind if I braid your hair, Vienna? I've been researching how to do it. No citizen from this planet has hair like yours."

"Sure." I'm not sure why I said it or why I'm at such ease with those I've met on this planet instead of my own. It's as if I've finally been accepted into one of the popular groups that I was ostracized from on Earth. She responds with a smile, tapping her fingers together. I turn away from her so she can reach my hair. As she begins running her fingers through it, I feel guilty. Mom never touched my hair, as far back as I can remember. She taught me how to manage it myself at an early age. The tingling in my scalp soothes me like signing with Harper. Which is weird because normally touch seems the opposite to me.

Theopat even gossips with me a bit. "The fashion on this planet's nothing like what you have on Earth. Can you tell me about some of the clothing you've worn?"

"I'm not the best person to fill you in on that. I'm pretty plain and stick to what is almost a uniform, so I don't have to make too many choices."

"But why not, you have so many options available to you."

"I guess I'm most comfortable in jeans, a small tee, and a zip up hoodie."

"But your body would fit any style."

"Ha, most girls on Earth like a little more voluptuous body than I have. I'm so tall and gangly."

"But that's perfect. Any style would work on you, just cinch in the material."

"Thank you, Theopat. I like the way you think." Maybe I

would do all right on Planet Vortex if my dad were able to take over the facility.

The lights flicker off and on. "Oh, time for your procedure. I'll check in with you from time to time. I want to hear more about Planet Earth." Theopat says goodbye as she heads back to the elevator.

Adorned with my first braid, my shoulder's readily available for the apheresis catheter. A nurse with the same mallard-shaped head administers a local numbing agent after wiping my skin with an alcohol swab. I notice an aloe smell. That must be their water replacement. Though I can't feel the pain of the insertion piercing my skin, I can feel the tug and pull of the tissue. Anesthesia might not work but numbing does. I look at Al and Viscerous, who are reading articles on tablets, totally bored by the procedure.

"How did you access articles?" I ask.

"You're free to search online here," Viscerous answers.

No need to hack firewalls, as they do not seem to exist here as they do at the facility. I wonder how many times Al and Viscerous have been here.

"So, what happens while we're here?" I ask Viscerous.

"Exactly what's happening now, over and over again. Better request an extra blanket and pillow. You more than likely will get cold with the extraction process. We're going to be here a while."

I follow his instructions and both things are brought immediately, but then I hear beeping and loud voices. I look over at Al to see what's going on. Blood's squirting out of his shoulder like a water balloon with a pinprick hole. Multiple staff head in his direction as his nurse attempts to hold gauze on the entry point. Viscerous stands, "Damn it, the bionic limbs have caused stronger blood flow. Al shouldn't even be here."

I try to stretch my free arm across my cot to Al, but the

needle won't allow that. Al's always looking out for others, but for the first time, I see fear for himself in his eyes. That's when an Earthquake fault line ruptures in my heart. Now my pull to Al is as strong as the one to save my dad. The bleeding won't stop because they haven't removed the needle. "You have to take that out. He won't stop bleeding until you do." I point to the needle while talking to the staff who completely ignore me.

Now Viscerous isn't only standing but has pulled his own needle out. He walks over to Al and removes the needle gouging into Al's shoulder the way I'd feared the vulture's talons would in mine when it saved me from the hot spot. After Viscerous has removed the needle, and the staff stops Al's bleeding, the flame-throwing guard appears. I hadn't noticed him among the numerous cots, but I guess he's been here all along. "Step away from the patient. Orders are to resume without disruption."

As the flame-throwing guard lifts his club, Viscerous grabs it, rendering the guard useless. "If procedures continue, Cromwell will be down a study specimen, and he'll be upset with you."

The guard's arm muscles constrict, but it's useless against Viscerous' grip on the club.

"I think regular intravenous tubes will suffice for him," I spout out. "His blood flows stronger. You won't need the apheresis catheter." As the staff inserts an I.V. on the other shoulder and everything flows smoothly, they turn to me and smile.

My own nurse puts her hand on my cheek and says, "Thank you."

With that, everyone returns to normal, but the flame-throwing guard's staring Viscerous down. I'm afraid to think what this could mean.

For the next hour, nurses are moving about collecting bags and putting the contents into an apheresis machine.

I allow myself to lie down and watch the separation of stem cells from the blood. Luckily, my free hand is on Al's side. I reach my hand out to him. Since they had to switch arms, his free hand is on my side too. Even with all the hustle and bustle going on, I'm able to treasure his hand holding mine although my fingers are becoming numb from the procedure. Al's lips are beginning to turn blue, but it's as if he's the gravity keeping me centered. I can't believe we're going to endure days of this treatment. Sometime within the following hour, I drift asleep. Nightmares of the flame-throwing guard attacking Viscerous appear instantly. Fire swarms his skin in these dreams, and the unprotected arteries melt as red paints his body from head to toe.

I awaken to the sound of an alarm and look at the clock surprised by the time that's passed. Then I quickly turn to Al to see if he's sputtering blood again, but he's just waking. There's nothing wrong with him apart from the bluish color of his lips. An overhead announcement begins. I'm getting pretty tired of announcements.

"Nephilim staff, we have to close the hollow blinds. An unscheduled shuttle has breached Planet Vortex atmosphere. This is a code blue. Repeat code blue."

The staff hurries to turn off the lights and press the buttons releasing the blinds hiding the light from the many moons. We're enveloped in darkness. I recognize her voice as Theopat enters the room.

"First time we've had a real code blue and not just a drill. Who do you think it is?" she asks my nurse.

Murmuring begins throughout the cots and then grows louder.

"Better release the fireflies to keep this room calm," the nurse tells Theopat.

Theopat presses a button, and the room falls into a hush apart from a few gasps, one being my own. The walls become alive as dots of rainbow fly around us. Al squeezes my hand, and we both sit up. Somehow, the colorful glow makes his eyes more fascinating than ever.

"Theopat, how'd you do this?" I ask.

"One of the meteors that dropped water on the planet brought firefly larvae with it. We've been able to maintain them but changed them with altered luciferin molecules. That's how you see the colors before you. Isn't it amazing?"

Al gets a firefly to land on his finger, and we both stare at it. That's when I overhear the nurse whispering to Theopat. "They say that a boarding employee at the Earth liftoff site recognized a defunct identification. The individual claimed things about his university that he later found to be untrue. He looked into the person's claim and discovered they had used false identification."

As I try to lean in and hear the nurse better, I take one look back at Al. His eyebrows are raised as he mouths, "Is this concerning you?"

Guess he was able to hear the whispering as well as I had. I nod my head and release my hand from his to hold a finger to my mouth.

"The guy believes it is not only dangerous for the imposter to be here, but harmful for the medical facility," the nurse continues.

Prickles of sensation cover my arm that has the catheter as if I'm losing feeling. I'm going to need to check to be sure my cover's not blown. At least, I'm away from the place of torture, the place where the boarding employee will be looking. I remember him saying "next" as if it was just an hour ago and his asking about Dr. Bobek. I knew it had been a mistake to mention my teacher's name.

The nurse and Theopat get up to make rounds, and I don't get to hear any more of their conversation.

"Are you okay?" Al whispers to me.

"Yeah," I say.

What if they figured out exactly who I am and why I'm here? What if they try to talk to my dad? What would Cromwell do to silence him? Is he in danger and I'm stuck here unable to do anything to help or even warn him?

"You're shaking. What's going on?" Al asks.

"We need to get back."

"I don't think that would be in your best interest right now."

"My dad!"

He brushes some of the hair strands that have escaped the braid away from my face. Then he kisses me on the forehead.

"Hey, it's going to be okay. Your dad's a smart man."

I get up and scoot my cot next to his. We embrace the best we can around the stem cell harvest tubing.

"Are you sure?" I ask wanting desperately to believe Dad will be all right.

"Yes! Plus, Albina would find a way to get word to us if it wasn't."

I'm able to calm down a bit with this information. Then I take a deep breath and look at it another way. What if it's only the boarding employee? What if he's afraid he'll lose his job if he allowed the wrong person to board so he's only here for me? But what will he do then when he doesn't find me? I need to let it go for now. There's nothing I can do except raise flags by attempting to get back to the facility to protect dad. I need to relax so I don't do that.

Luckily, I find a qualified distraction. Being next to Al's body is as comforting as the teddy bear I kept far beyond the age of stuffed animals. Yet, I'm excited too.

He softly brushes his hand up my arm and the particles of my skin explode with every touch. My peach fuzz arm hairs rise to follow where his hand leads. As he continues, my breathing finally slows down. It's as if I'm crashing from a forty-eight-hour shift. Every muscle he touches tightens at first but eventually calms. Remarkably, for the first time since before I found out about my acceptance into the medical facility, I fall asleep easily without any nightmares or dreams.

When I awake, the blinds have been removed and bright sunlight shines in on us all. My face is right next to Al's. He's looking at me as though he's been staring for hours. He puts his hand softly on the back of my neck and his forehead against mine. "Vienna, how'd I go so long without you?"

"I don't know. I wish you'd found me much earlier."

"Did you know you murmur in your sleep?"

"What? Did I say anything?"

"I couldn't make out much, but I think I heard my name a couple of times."

His smug grin makes me blush. I can only imagine what I said.

"Tsk, tsk, tsk," Theopat approaches us. "Your cots should not be this close."

At first I'm afraid, caught in the usual medical facility orderly fear of punishment. Theopat wears a friendly smile as if she's been allowed to hear a secret. She must see my look of concern though because her face turns into one of worry.

"I was just kidding around, sweetheart. You two are adorable."

Al and I both sit up and straighten our disheveled hair.

The nurse comes around and asks me to rise so she can put my cot back in its rightful place. Theopat pulls her aside and begins whispering. "The shuttle's gone. I guess Cromwell convinced them that it all had been a mistake. You know how he likes to be private."

My eyes dart from the two in hushed conversation to Al and then back. I feel as though with every heartbeat there's fear and love. Thump, what does Cromwell know? Thump, I slept next to someone I care more for every day. Thump, that was a close one! Thump, did he stay awake and watch me the entire time?

Meals are brought around to us, and we all dive in as if we haven't eaten in days. It reminds me of when I met Al. I'd been surprised at his hunger, but now my own echoes his. Theopat sits next to me and asks more Earth questions.

"What are people like on Earth? I see so many artistic talents from the planet, yet I hear about wars and people starving."

"It depends on where you live. Areas are different economically. The art is spectacular, I guess, but I tend to stick to science and mechanics."

"Oh, tell me about mechanics. I hear you can travel about with only magnetic polarization."

If only I'd allowed Vex to travel with me, claiming he was a lab partner. He could've produced such beautiful images for Theopat. I try to dig into my memory to find something that will amuse her. Some of the girls on the Olympiad team came up with magic tricks to pass the time between competitions. They'd hide one coin while showing another seeming to produce a coin from thin air over and over. I find a round plastic piece about the size of a coin. Luckily, I've practiced the trick before as it takes time to perfect. I try to perform the act with Theopat, and she giggles. I think I overlooked a couple of steps, but she's smiling and enthralled with trying to perform the trick too, so I don't think she minds.

The nurse comes around to begin the harvesting process again. I look at Al, whose lips have regained their color, and wonder how long it'll be before they turn blue. Then, I look at Viscerous to see how he's holding up. That's when I first notice the electric handcuff on his free arm connected to one of the cot bars. If they were able to cuff Viscerous without my noticing could I have also missed communication from

Albina? Viscerous looks at me and shrugs. "You two have a good evening?"

"Yeah, but why are you cuffed, Viscerous?"

"Appears the guard didn't approve of my stepping in."

"No," Al says. "Man, why didn't you say something sooner."

"You two were enjoying the moment. I didn't want to intrude. What can they do to me that surpasses my artery alteration?"

I look at Al. His nostrils expand and then retract as he takes a deep breath. I look at Viscerous. He's completely calm and in no fear of being bound. The look is so relaxed that I think he knows what he might face and has come to peace with it. The pinpricks in my arm rise to my throat and then to my head. I close my eyes to get a grip on things, but all I see on the back of my eyelids is Viscerous' eyes. They're the eyes of someone about to run through fire to save a person he loves. It haunts me even more than the waterfall of blood from Rigled.

My worry subsides as we all continue in the stem cell harvesting. Everyone around us seems bored out of their minds. Stuck in the same spot, I guess you can only focus for so long before tiring. Many people nap throughout the day and I find myself catching catnaps too. My sleeping patterns have been anything but normal recently. The guard has to uncuff Viscerous when he needs to use the restroom. Nurses would not comply when the guard had demanded Viscerous be catheterized. They claimed it was an unnecessary procedure as Viscerous is an able-bodied man. As the flame-throwing guard returns Viscerous to the cuffs and departs, Theopat sits next to Viscerous, and I overhear their hushed conversation.

"Some from outside can assist your movement when the time is right. I just don't think it will be right until everyone falsely accused has their name cleared," Theopat says.

"How have the attempts been going?"

"Every time we get a case to trial, Cromwell's attorney sabotages it with continuations and additional charges from alleged crimes at the facility."

"I see. That does make things more difficult. What's his attorney's name?"

A nurse comes by to collect more bags for the apheresis machine. Viscerous and Theopat quickly change the subject.

"So there's no way I can order any salmon?" Viscerous asks Theopat.

The nurse interrupts, "Theopat, bed six needs a blanket."

"No, afraid we don't have that available. Let me see if I can get you something else for a snack," Theopat answers as she walks away.

I pull up my tablet. Since Al and Viscerous were able to access articles, I attempt to access my makeshift 3-D sand printer. There's enough sand available for three rungs so I program it to operate on its own. While it runs I begin researching any articles I can find on court cases to clear guards' names. Theopat was right. Luckily, the World Government have made a universal legal system. Case after case, they've been unsuccessful. Everything from insufficient evidence to prove innocence to political pressures causing a judge to be unable to allow the hearing. Wow, Cromwell must really be connected within this planet's government, but I can't find the name of his attorney anywhere. How else would it have been so easy to bring false charges against individuals? I even find an article about a lawyer being charged with contempt after yelling a slew of curses at a judge. It's no surprise to find out that he wound up at the facility too.

Theopat heads my direction and I close the articles. She begins putting my hair into a different braid. Once the nurses have left our area, I begin speaking.

"Theopat, is it true what you were saying to Viscerous?"

"Yes, darling, unfortunately it is."

"How do you know so much about it? Do you know someone in the government who could help?"

"I wish I did. I've been researching every case since my..."

She hesitates and looks around to be sure the nurses can't hear us.

"Since your what, Theopat?"

"Since they took my brother and made him a guard."

"Oh no, I'm so sorry. Is everyone affected by the facility on Vortex?"

"It seems like only those of us without connection to the government are affected. I try to send messages to him, but it's very difficult. In the last message I received he said he wasn't able to sleep because of the nightmares."

"I know what he means."

"Yes, I'm sorry you've been sucked into this too. I hope you're able to escape before anything bad happens."

The nurses have returned and we're unable to continue. Since my back is to them, I put my right fist over my chest. Theopat smiles before walking away.

Al and I scoot our cots next to each other when the lights are out again.

"How are you holding up?" he asks me.

"Do you really think your plan can work?"

"Are you talking about the mutiny?" he asks in a whisper.

"What else would I be talking about?" I ask.

"We'd target Cromwell while he's in one of his secret labs."

"Wouldn't he just call for the guards to attack?"

"We'd shut down communications."

"What do you plan to do once you have Cromwell captive? Don't you think the government would step in and free him? Things would just get worse."

"The plan is still developing. We have to do something."

"I know."

"How about you let me enjoy sleeping outside of isolation?" He wraps his arms around me. The arms that were not the ones he had when he arrived on this planet. Yet even with all of his limbs removed, he seems to have the strongest will in the fight. I watch him sleep this time. His eyelids flutter once he's in REM sleep. He must be dreaming. I wonder what he's dreaming about.

14

TAKEN

Vienna

As Colsam returns us to the facility, I see an impending wall of gray muscle. I can spot their weapons, fully activated and ready for an attack. The guards' bodies are so similar they appear to be clones until closer examination reveals individual characteristics. Some have different-shaped ears and eyes, and not all of them are the same shade of gray. This is the armor of the one true enemy. Eyes like the lenses of binoculars and telescopes. Beak-like lips that whisper about our activities to the head surgeon. Yet, I wonder if more stand out behaviorally among them, like my dad among the scientists.

The triangle appears to have a few aberrations. If my dad believes he can save this situation against all odds, I ponder what these irregularities mean. Could they possibly see that their leader is corrupt and it's worth it to fight him? Do we have a few more on our side?

When we approach a couple of guards step forward. I'm frozen in fear as they approach me. They're unstoppable like an exploding star. They did figure me out. What if they're here to arrest me and take me back to Earth...*without* Dad. Too bad I don't have the shuttle built yet. I could at least make a run for it and report everything that's occurring here.

But they pass by me and step next to Viscerous. The flame-throwing guard puts him in handcuffs. That's when Dr. Cromwell walks out from behind the triangle. "This man attempted to sabotage studies. He's to be arrested until I've decided on proper punishment."

Colsam steps next to Viscerous. "He only tried to save a life. He wasn't trying to corrupt the study. Just take a look at the Nephilim footage, you'll see." Theopat must have informed him about what happened.

"That's enough. Do not undermine me in front of others, Colsam. This is your final warning." Dr. Cromwell lifts his chin toward a guard who then lunges forward and punches Colsam in the gut.

Colsam lets out a cough as he bends forward, looking at Dr. Cromwell with pure hatred.

"We've had to increase security after the unscheduled shuttle," Cromwell says. "Nothing can go unpunished." Cog it! Does he know? Maybe revolution isn't too bad. Could we recruit enough right here and now? Perhaps we'd have an advantage being in the open. Perhaps Aviator could help. It wouldn't matter that vultures are chipped once we've overthrown Cromwell.

The guards escort us into the facility where we meet a new physician. Dr. Bargory House has been making news with his medical findings. I wonder how he ended up here. Then I realize why he might have been hired. Are they trying to replace my dad? Did he travel aboard the unscheduled shuttle? That seems pretty convenient. What communication channels does Cromwell have set up? After that, they bring us to our lab. Albina's there. She looks behind us for Viscerous, but when the door shuts she looks at us. Then she crumples to the floor. "What happened? Where is he?"

Al and I sit down on either side of her and explain what happened at Nephilim and when we returned. We hold her hands when she begins crying.

"He would've wanted this over another experiment, to be punished for saving someone he cares for. He's such a good man," Albina says despite a shaky ribcage.

"Yes, he is," we respond in unison.

"I should've seen something like this happening," Albina says softly, rubbing tears away from her blotchy face, color appearing despite her usual lack of pigmentation. "I've been worried since the shuttle. Security's been heightened. We're escorted everywhere we go now."

"You mean they're escorting us to labs and everything again?" Al says.

She nods.

"How are we going to revolt in increased security?" Al asks. "How can we save Viscerous?"

We attempt to continue our studies to keep up pretenses, but I find it difficult to concentrate. As I'm researching the next non-bio body, visions of Viscerous holding the flame-throwing guard's arm resurface in my mind. I actually smile.

"What's there to smile about?" Al asks me.

"I was just thinking about Viscerous' strong arm holding the club."

"He's such a vigorous man," Albina says with her head down.

I drown myself in the study. My new non-bio body patient has already been seen once and doesn't have any signs of epilepsy. The thought allows Charlie's memory to resurface. When I tap the screen to pull up her records, I find that she experienced a seizure while I'd been away at Nephilim. Is she okay? How's her family handling it? I look at Al, and his eyelashes touch his eyebrows as he looks up, feeling my gaze with a sixth sense. Tears attempt to surface as I think about how my getting closer to him could cause him harm.

When we're escorted to the cafeteria, I try to distance myself from Al but he's not allowing that. He stays close to me no matter where I go. Approaching the doors feels like the first day here. I wait for Rigled's rough voice and then remember that it no longer exists. Al walks through the line with me. I don't even look at the food. When we turn to our usual table, I find my legs turning to jello beneath me. Al nudges me forward as I stare at my dad sitting at our table.

I walk to the table and whisper, "Dad, what are you doing here?" I look around to be sure the guards aren't close enough to hear us.

"I get to have a meal with you again, Sierra. Come on, have a seat by your old man."

"Sierra?" Al asks, raising an eyebrow at me.

"Yeah, that's my real name," I whisper trying to promote Al and Dad to whisper too.

"Why didn't you tell me?"

"Guess I just got used to Vienna. Oh, Dad, this is Al. He's my uh…" suddenly I'm at a loss for words.

"Lab-mate." Al extends his bionic hand to my dad for a shake. "Sir, it is an honor to officially meet. You saved my life." Lab-mate? Not friend? Ha, a part of me had yearned for him to say boyfriend. I've never had a boyfriend before. Even in the midst of turmoil, I find myself wanting to squeal like some of the girls from my school or scroll "I love Al" in my digital journal. I need to focus on why my dad's suddenly allowed to eat with the rest of us. Lab-mate's perfect.

"Good to officially meet you." My dad shakes Al's hand

with the unabashed friendliness I usually exhibit. Maybe that was a characteristic he passed down to me.

Albina looks at me expectantly. "Dad, this is Albina."

"A pleasure to meet you." My dad shakes her hand.

"You saved my Viscerous during his procedure. I'm indebted to you."

I introduce him to Yesha, who looks at my dad as if he's the perfect role model. I find myself proud, even if I'm not completely in sync with her intentions. I also introduce him to Pixie. She doesn't understand everything but is kind, a natural characteristic for her even after the brain matter transplant. My dad hugs me before we sit and eat. It's like a holiday meal I should have had as a child. Despite being surrounded by heartbreak, this is the kind of experience I've yearned for. I'm surrounded by people close to me here. I sit back and listen to my dad talk of studies with everyone. His eyes light up when he mentions his newest finding. He's found a way to move conscience and memory into non-bio bodies without any defects. My heart flutters with this finding. He closed the gap in study before I was able to.

"So does that mean Cromwell will choose non-bios over live subjects now?" I ask him when everyone else is lost in conversation over the new findings.

"Cromwell still believes the essence of human nature resides in live hosts," my dad says. "Why do you think he forced me to step down? I could no longer follow his studies on people when we have a perfect alternative. I'm general population to him now, no longer his right hand."

So maybe now my dad will leave this place. He no longer will be able to help save people here if he's demoted, right. "So, he won't use non-bio bodies to save Sorna and Damien ever. Will he?" I ask.

My dad drops his fork and stops eating.

"So, the study on non-bio bodies is merely a cover, isn't it?"

"You shouldn't know so much. I should've found a way to get you on the non-scheduled shuttle. Don't trust him, Sierra."

I look around and notice the number of guards watching us has doubled. They're almost a completely uninterrupted line against the wall, no spaces between them. As the flame-throwing guard announces that it's time to head to our quarters, yelling so that people will listen, my dad clenches me in a sideways hug. This kind of hug is like one from a friend, not the warm, bear hug he used to give me as a child. It feels like he doesn't want to let go. Unfortunately, he's missed many years. I'm no longer a child. It's not his responsibility to protect me anymore. I briefly hug him back and then head to line up at the red door. I'm going to have to distance myself from him even though that's the last thing I want to do. I have to get closer to Cromwell and Dad's not going to hear of that.

In my quarters, I'm again unable to fall asleep. I grab the portable tablet, set the 3-D sand printer to print one more rung while hoping the wind pushed more sand closer, and begin searching local news. There's a blocker installed that I have to navigate around but superseding the technology shield is something I've conquered before. The main headlines seem to promote the medical facility and its findings. There's even an interview with a child about how the facility saved his arm. Part of me wants to stop there. The news doesn't mention that the facility freely takes the arms of involuntary subjects.

I urge myself forward, skipping through to hopefully find someone out there with a sense for what's really going on. I notice articles about other planets Cromwell's approaching for study. Not another medical facility! I stop at the obituaries. There's one of a defense attorney for the facility staff that catches my eye. This man had lost virtually every case but a week before his death he found success. He was able to clear someone of all charges. I try to think back to see if I can remember a guard that was freed, but nothing pops into my mind. The defense attorney died at a young age from burning, though no clear evidence for the cause of the nuclear fusion fire could be found.

The foldable tablet shuts down before I can read more. All of the incubator lights turn off including mine. I guess the increased security includes a lights-out time. I haven't even changed into pajamas or brushed my teeth. How will I continue my building? I walk to my hammock avoiding sharp objects as I've memorized my small room. When I settle in, I imagine Harper and me testing oxygen pills. Then I think about Mom. Kitchen and Vex will be assisting her, but what can she be thinking? I've never been away more than a day without speaking to her. Now she's without Dad and me both. What could be going through her mind? What would she do if she were called to court to give a psychological profile of someone she knew was being wrongly accused?

I breathe in, feeling my lungs stretch as far as they can. I breathe out until my chest is compressed, imagining a large, dark circle. Within it forms a violet circle and inside that a blue one. I inhale and exhale again before green, red and yellow circles form. There they freeze and oxygen exchanges without thinking. Finally, the last circle expands like the sun expanding toward the Earth. I drift to sleep.

At breakfast, Cromwell has the flame-throwing guard collect me for a meeting again. "Vienna, there's ground-breaking study going on requiring your assistance. Given your specialty, Cromwell's inclined to hear your opinion."

My dad stands with me this time. "I can be of help. Why don't I join you?"

"I'm sorry, Dr. Perierat, Cromwell says, these findings are strictly within Vienna's avenue," the guard says as he gestures toward another guard. The second guard approaches my dad, and my head throbs in fear as if someone beat it against a cement wall over and over again.

"Thank you, Septimus." I put my hand on his arm, obscuring the guard's approach. "I can handle this." I look into those hazel eyes and it feels as if I'm going through an allergy test, multiple needles poking into my back. I squeeze his arm and turn away before my resolve can fail me. He takes a seat and the guard backs off, but as I walk away, I see my dad grip his hair and then run his hand over his face, pulling his cheeks down before holding his chin.

"Vienna, time is of the essence since the unscheduled shuttle. I can't let anyone intercede before I've found a way to revive Sorna and Damien," Cromwell tells me as we walk through the holographic hallway.

"Don't you have pull on other planets too?"

"Well, yes, how'd you know about that? Never mind, it doesn't matter. They don't have much time. I have them in cryogenic sleep in a Planet Vortex satellite hotel."

"Oh," is all I can muster back. That does change things.

"We need to speed up studies. I may need you in the lab more, oh and uh, I'm going to need to test you a couple days early. Is that all right?"

He's actually asking permission. "Sure, I guess. What else do I have to do while stuck here?" Even though I answer unenthusiastically, I find myself curious about the science of his family. "So how were you able to get them into cryogenic sleep after the beak plunges through their bodies?"

"Ah, I was wondering when you'd ask that," he said as he grips his hands together, as if concocting the most splendid scheme. "We had to resuscitate them when they returned to the facility, but as their hearts began beating again, we were able to introduce cryonics before their memories and personalities drifted off."

Now I ask the question that's really been plaguing me. "Why would live hosts differ from non-bio bodies free of altercation? I understand that clones would merely replicate the beak injured versions and be ineffective but non-bio bodies wouldn't have that issue."

"Few have studied the longevity of the non-bios without deflection as that has just recently been discovered, but I have. I found non-deflection before Dr. Perierat and the results after five years show atrophy within the DNA."

He found this long before my dad if he's been able to study the aftermath five years out. So what had his questions to the attending physician about non-bios meant? My dad was probably unable to give the research the attention it needed with Dr. Cromwell's mutations. He's probably had to set many studies aside. I wonder if it was an earlier study by my dad that gave Cromwell the key. "Have you found possible solutions to the atrophy?"

"Yes, but those studies are inconclusive. Sometimes reinsertion of memory has saved the DNA, but other times not. Stem cells have played a key role, but not without a few errors."

Then it hits me, why is he disclosing such information to me. Why did he approach me at a time of need? He needs me, but who am I among the multiple specialists in this area?

Cromwell must see my look of discouragement. "I only mention to you the importance of the situation as a few of the procedures about to occur may dishearten you. I'll need those test results in five days. I hope you'll be compliant."

"Uh, what procedures?"

"I can't divulge them now. I'm afraid your lack of assistance would cause harm to those around you."

I want to scream! I want a relic cannon, so I can load it and blow a hole through his chest.

"I'll try my best."

As he waves his hand at me in dismissal, I venture back through the holograph hallway. A few feet depict what an x-ray of my body would, my teeth and bones making stronger white lines. Another few feet depict my body temperature. My brain and heart in the scan radiate a vibrant red. The last section shows psychological readings halfway down the back of my skull and to the right light up in a bright crimson color. Apparently, I have been practicing the art of deception, but to who and what for, the scan cannot tell.

When I walk into my lab, Al and Albina don't interrupt themselves from their studies. Are they upset with me getting closer to Cromwell? I continue my study on the next non-bio body, knowing it's in vain. How can I continue this study knowing that a process has been found to rid deflection? Was it administered here? Could we keep someone from going through what Charlie did?

"Al, have the new findings been administered to these non-bios?"

He clears his throat as if someone has just choked him. "No, V...Sierra, they have not. Just continue the study, so we're not punished."

He must detest my episodes with Cromwell.

Albina makes a sad, sideways smirk, "Thought you'd catch on before too long. Cromwell is worse than a demon."

If they think Cromwell is worse than Satan as he tries to save his family, what do they think of me overriding revolution and planned assassination in order to free my dad?

"I heard you taught Theopat about Earth," Albina interjects in an attempt to break through the tension.

"Yeah, she's something else, isn't she?"

"She reminds me of Colsam," Al adds. "I know she'd be all for a revolution with her constituents being falsely accused."

Of late I haven't been entirely against mutiny, but I still don't like the thought of losing anyone. "What do you know about the weapons here?"

"What do you mean?" Albina asks.

"How do they run?"

"Which weapon are you talking about?" Al asks.

"All of them. If we could find a way to stop them from operating perhaps a coup wouldn't necessarily lead to bloodshed."

"See, I knew you'd come around," he says.

I roll my eyes.

"I'll look into it," Albina says.

I'm tired of looking into non-bio information I know will not be used. Instead, I search for flaws within live hosts but, according to the data, Cromwell's worked out most of the kinks. There's still one though. Rejection possibilities have not been fully eliminated.

An overhead announcement begins like an early alarm clock ring that one would like to hit snooze in response to, "Members of the medical facility, punishment has been scheduled for a resident. The proceedings will occur in three days."

Albina drops to the ground sobbing as Al punches a non-human factor chair. The chair falls to the floor.

"We'll find a way around this," I try to soothe them both. I walk up to Al and rub his shoulder as he had mine, realizing that distancing from him is impossible while we're held captive. When his tearful eyes meet my own, I lose my composure and begin crying myself. We approach Albina and hold her in a strong embrace. There's only one punishment they can be speaking of.

15
PLAN

Vienna

AT DINNER, I APPROACH THE OTHER SIDE OF THE cafeteria and notice a mural has been rolled into the room. I wonder who painted it. The painting has scenery from past lives. A pasture with cows blends into a city like my own. Grain storage bins turn into tall buildings. Computer-programmed tractors into floating cars. Even the cornstalks blend into bendable solar panels on rooftops in an aerial view. Funny how everything seems to fit together. If only that could be the way it works in real life.

I wonder if Cromwell's trying to promote peace with this new artwork. Like that could work. I invite Quintus and Lucretia to sit at our table. Their wounds are almost healed. Quintus' arms are no longer wrapped in gauze and bandages and do not cover the left side of Lucretia's face anymore. They hold hands throughout the entire meal as if the connection can keep them from ever being separated again.

"How are the non-bio body studies going, Al?" Quintus asks.

"Our lab's making great headway, but you should talk to Septimus about his newest finding."

Quintus looks at my dad, "What did you find?".

"I've discovered a way to eliminate deflection. Similar to the robotic bloodstream inhibitors that kill viruses. I've made ones that can help adapt the nerves and vessels of a non-bio body. The most common place for deflection is within the brain, as that's where the conscience and memories are implanted. That is why there's been such a high percentage of seizures. The inhibitors will eventually need to adapt every part of the non-bio, using cells from the body of the conscience and memory donor. This can be done successfully, but the process will need to be repeated to avoid atrophy of the DNA. Since non-bio bodies don't undergo the same cycle of life, eventually there will always be deflection. An aging adaptation process can be induced by the robots. I haven't been able to complete my studies as Cromwell has demoted me and removed me from my lab."

I can't help but smile, hearing my dad rant. I remember how he used to go on and on about his studies at the dinner table at home. Equipment and notes would be strewn about his home office like a tornado had gone through, for months and months at a time. He'd always complain about how things weren't working, and theories were proving incorrect. Until he finally found what he was searching for. Then his composure would calm, and organization would revisit his office. His conversations would change, as if he could only carry on confidently after successful experiments. Right now, the light in his eyes is a half twinkle. He's unable to draw a complete conclusion and seeing him imbalanced leaves gashes in my insides.

"That's great, Septimus," Lucretia says as she squeezes Quintus' hand. When I first heard these two aboard the shuttle, they'd creeped me out. I see them for who they really are now. Like many of us here, they don't want any of this. Cromwell was forcing them to tattoo no matter how much they might object being a means to his end. A thought pops into my head again: who else received a tattoo?

"Will Cromwell use non-bio bodies now?" Quintus asks.

My dad shakes his head. "Why do you think I've been demoted?"

I watch their faces turn back to the sad ones many seem to carry here, eyes like the hollows of caves. As they push their food around in disappointment, I recall what Cromwell told me. He must have lied when he claimed to have known how to rid non-bios of deflection. He wouldn't have made the comment about atrophy if he'd been speaking of the robotic bloodstream inhibitors Dad discovered. Why would he lie to me about it? People here know he prefers live bodies. I wonder what else he's been lying about.

"Will you return to shuttle assignment when the next one lands?" Albina asks Lucretia.

"We too have been demoted. It's just as well. I don't think we'd be ready for responsibility in five days."

"I'm sorry to hear about that," Albina says. "I know you two love flying."

"We're just happy to have each other," Quintus says looking at Lucretia, who looks down and rubs her thumb on his hand.

"We're sorry about Viscerous," she says to Albina.

"Thank you." Albina lowers her head, chewing on the inside of her cheek.

"I still say we need to revolt or kill Cromwell," Yesha finally speaks up, sitting taller.

"What in the world are you talking about, dear?" my dad asks her.

"You should be the one running this place instead of him, Septimus."

He smiles. "While that's an intriguing thought, we can't put people in danger."

She slumps a little. She looks up to my dad, but certainly disagrees with what he just said.

Thoughts stir around in my head, and light disrupts the darkness I've been feeling, like when you mix water with citric acid and zinc sulfide, creating a glow in a dark, bubbling solution. Maybe I can do something.

"Quintus, where'd they keep you before they brought you to the classroom?" I ask.

"Why would you ask that?"

"Just curious."

"It's one of the most secure sectors. Near the front entry of the facility, there's a hallway with windowed labs and a hallway to the right. Eventually the hallway on the right circles around back to the cafeteria, but before that, there are three doors requiring fingerprint and retina scans to grant access. I was held in the room behind the second door."

I can't recall ever being in that section of the building. I've only been between the front door and the cafeteria via the other path (plus the tunnels don't seem to go there). Even Cromwell's quarters are within the section I've been in. I wonder which of the three doors Viscerous is behind. I bet it's the second like Quintus.

The flame-throwing guard announces for everyone to line up at the red door. Without Rigled's brash voice, the effect isn't the same. People continue their conversations and remain seated. The guard fires his club in the air. All talking stops as everyone stares at the flames. Every other guard approaches a table. With that, we all stand and line up. I keep hoping things will get better here, but they just seem to be getting worse and worse.

Quickly, before lights-out, I check the 3-D Sand printer sensors. I'm able to program it to continue building rungs, pushing the ladder up and over the wall with a couple bends. I'm able to alter the code so that it will automatically build as soon as sand avails and pause when it runs out until the ladder's complete. It's not near as far as I'd like to take it (shuttles) but it may come in handy at some point in time.

That night, I have a dream. It's a different time, about a hundred or so years ago based on the brick buildings and our clothing. My own clothes are like a costume one might choose at an old-fashioned black and white multidimensional prism photography studio. Al's in my dream too, but with all of his original limbs intact. Even now, he causes my heart rate to quiver. It is night, and the old clothes are dark. Al's picking a lock, which is something not as easily tackled with the newer digital locks. He grabs my hand and leads me into the building and then motions behind me.

When I look back, I see a younger Viscerous and Albina. Viscerous is a normal man with arteries where they should be, and Albina has dark, olive skin with hot chocolate colored eyes. They join us in the building. Viscerous goes to a computer. There's a plastic screen that he turns on. They haven't existed for at least fifty years. When I look around, I see that we're in a medical lab. I can't even escape labs in my dreams! Albina and I walk to a refrigerator, but when she opens the door I feel sweltering heat instead of coldness.

I rub my eyes. What was that? It all seemed so real. I look around to get my bearings back but when I spot the open rectangle in my incubator, I inhale sharply. The door's open. How did that happen? I hear flapping and fluttering. Then I see my vulture flying above. It dives down perfectly. When it lands on the hill next to me, I feel like a child again. I climb out of the incubator and onto its back, petting its neck.

"It's so nice to see you again, Aviator. How'd you know the door would be open?"

The vulture moves its head around, pointing at every incubator. They're all open. I look around to see if any guards will catch us. Colsam's at the podium outside the red door. When I look at him, he salutes me. I smile back. Thank you, Colsam! Flying from my incubator feels like when the shuttle lifted off, back when I believed I could rescue Dad. Rising above the hill and facility, I can see the wall that surrounds us. In the clouds again, my mind races. I pet the vulture.

"Do you think you could show me the other side of the facility? Or would the chip stop you?" The vulture points to its shoulder with its beak. I pet there and feel a scar in the perfect shape of a square. "You've removed your chip!" The vulture shakes her head up and down. Maybe we could escape on vultures.

We dip down, and I can see the roof of the facility. Flexible solar panels litter the space. When we near the opposite side, I spot a garage with railcars inside. The lights are on. I guess lights-out only occurs at our quarters. There's also a large shed, but the doors are closed so that I'm unable to see in. A field of some sort is built into the sand, like a training center. As we near the shed and turn around, I see three doors but no windows. The doors are an older style, not like the ones on computer-programmed sliders, and they open to the outside. I guess if they're meant to hold their residents captive, it makes sense that they don't open from within.

"Can we go lower to see the doors?"

The vulture moves its head side to side as if to tell me no. We rise back up over the roof and to the incubator side. My hands are shaking. I'd been so close to Viscerous but unable to do a thing. The vulture must sense my anxiety. It lifts up before making the dive down. I want to scream in delight as the wind sails through my hair but stay silent in order to not be caught.

The guards on the wall must've assumed it was just a vulture flying by our sleeping quarters. I don't know what they would do if they realized I was on its back. I don't want to return to my incubator, but Colsam whistles and the vulture lands. As I step in, the door resumes its place. I notice other scientists (Al, Albina, even my dad!) walking away from Colsam and returning to their incubators. Now the freedom I felt riding Aviator feels stripped, along with some of my trust. They knew exactly how to bait me to get me away!

After that, I'm fraught not with dreams, but nightmares. Instead of just roaming through labs, I'm now given visions of organ instead of limb transplants. I haven't seen organ transplant here before and in my dreams it's from a hundred years ago. Old plastic coolers surround me instead of cryogenic freezers. It's as if someone's trying to send vital information to me, but I'm unable to decipher the code.

In my lab the following day, it's just Al and myself.

"Albina didn't feel up to working," Al says. "She's using a sick day."

I realize this is the first time Al and I have been completely by ourselves. "'Viscerous' impending punishment is really getting to her, isn't it?" I ask.

"Um, yeah, with the heightened security, it's bound to be a harsher punishment," Al says.

I go to him and give him a hug this time. When he hugs me back, it's as if someone put sugar in my system through an I.V. I'm full of energy.

"Al, I read an article online about a kid who benefited from live limb transplants from the medical facility."

"You, what, how?"

"I'm somewhat capable of hacking into the system here, while it's running that is."

"So you could find the location," Al pauses for a bit before continuing. "Oh, who cares? Bionic limbs are stronger than organic ones. We should be focusing on something else."

"You know so much about me. You've met my dad. You know my 'real' name."

He rolls his eyes with that comment.

"But, what about you?" I've been yearning to know about him for so long, but we always seem to be surrounded by people and catastrophic events.

"My childhood was pretty boring. I don't think you'd be interested."

"Try me."

"Well, my parents died when I was seven. I kind of bounced through system after system until I made a life on my own. That's probably why I ended up here. The salary offered was far greater than anything I'd come across. I wanted to be financially independent."

"Do you remember anything about your parents?"

"I do, even though most people say that memories from that age wither away. I remember my mom growing a garden every year. I know our technology has made gardens somewhat unneeded, but my mom loved the sense of peace it gave her. Dad loved working on cars."

"That's beautiful, Al. I don't agree with what people say. I remember everything from my dad even though he was taken away from me at an early age. It's nice seeing him again."

"I wish I could see my parents. Sometimes it feels as though there's a piece of me that will never heal."

"You have Viscerous and Albina." I hold his arm, wanting to comfort him.

"Yeah for now at least, they're pretty good to me. I haven't told them about my parents, but I think they assume, since I don't speak of family at all. Part of me believes that once I have a family of my own, that unhealed piece will be smaller, know what I mean?" He looks at me and I am lost in his eyes.

"I think I do. I feel like part of me will be healed when my parents are back together, and we find my baby brother that I've never met. In fact, I just recently learned of his existence."

"You have a baby brother that you've never met. That's got to be difficult."

"Well, he's only six years or so younger than me so I guess I probably shouldn't refer to him as baby."

I look at him, knowing he understands me as I understand him. I remember when he first caught me and when he carried me from the tunnel. He has the courage to venture out into this planet. He has strength and determination that I admire. He had been upset the time Cromwell studied my intelligence, and this desire to protect me causes a warmth to embrace me. There's no way I can continue to distance myself from him. The pull I have to him is as strong as the polar streets back home, just with the magnets flipped. Instead of polar opposites pushing away from each other, Al's like the metal I would attract if I were a magnet, swift, strong, and unavoidable.

He puts his hand on my cheek, looking me in the eyes, "V...Sierra, I don't know what to call you."

"Can you please call me Sierra? It's my real name." I smile.

"Sierra, we haven't known each other very long, but I feel as though I've known you for ages." Then he moves his hand under my chin and lifts my head. As his lips touch mine, heat surges to my cheeks, chest, fingers, and everywhere. I could melt into a pool on the floor.

The lab door opens. "Ahem," Colsam coughs out.

Al and I pull away from each other. "Hi, Colsam," I say, blushing.

"Uh," Colsam takes a few steps in our direction, squares his shoulders, and lifts his head. "I came here to let you guys know that security's going to increase in a few days. Guards will be assigned to watch labs too."

"Really! Cromwell's going a little insane with all of this," Al says, holding my hand.

"Just wanted to give you a heads up," Colsam says, looking at our hands. Then he looks at me and his shoulders lower. He turns around with his head down and walks back to the door.

"Thank you, Colsam," I say.

I think I hear him mutter "No problem" as he leaves.

"Great, just what we need, more observation," Al says, grasping me into a hug.

"We should probably do some studying for the log." I don't want our conversation and kiss to end. We didn't even kiss completely. Al had just touched his lips to mine before we were interrupted.

"I guess," Al breathes out. He rolls his holograph screen next to mine. We sit next to each other, close enough so that we touch. "It feels like such a waste to continue these studies knowing they will not be used."

"I know, but I still find some parts interesting. Do you think I can get some of my dad's robotic bloodstream inhibitors to Charlie?"

"Possibly, why do you ask?"

"Charlie showed signs of epilepsy last time she was in here. I hid the findings because I didn't want to turn study away from non-bio bodies. Charlie experienced a seizure while we were at Nephilim. I need to help her."

"How'd you hide the findings?"

"I overrode the database."

He shakes his head, looking at me while biting his lower lip. I want to touch my lips to his again, but don't know how. Do people just jump in and kiss someone at any time?

"Here, I can show you where your Dad's study is in the system." He begins touching the screen, navigating through pages. I pull up Charlie's study on my own screen. "The method serial number's here, but we have to have approval to schedule it on Charlie's appointment conglomeration."

I copy the number from his screen into Charlie's sequence. As the approval request pops up, I find its location within the database. As I begin typing, the protection begins blocking me again, and the screen starts to disappear. I override as I did previously, but this time a password question pops onto the screen. It's one of the questions I answered incorrectly in the intelligence test. For some reason, the deep embedded fractional algebraic question seemed foggy in my brain. Now it's clear as a window freshly cleaned by robotic scrubbers. I'm able to move forward and schedule Charlie for an appointment. I wonder if I could somehow put her in my dad's care in the future.

"Wow, you could access so much with that ability."

"Well, I figured you knew since I was able to hack out of my quarters using these skills on the tablet to open my door and use Rigled's card." I half smile at him because I'm dreading what the additional password question means. Cromwell had been expecting me to make the move I just did and with my correct answer, he's partially received a second test without me being able to extract any further information from him.

"Oh, I just figured you'd obscure the door before it shut by placing your mat over it."

"You can do that?"

"Yeah, I do it all the time. The tricky part's not being caught by your escorting guard. I keep my mat right next to the door, and as the guard drives away, I put it at the top before the door closes entirely."

I smile at him and give him a hug before we continue our studies. Warmth comes over me when I touch him and allow a positive thought. Maybe I can still liberate Viscerous. I want to tell Al about my plan, but don't want to put him in danger and I'm afraid he'll try to stop me.

That night, I'm unable to use the mat to block the door from closing. I realize that in order to do so I'll have to deconstruct my hammock. Once I've untied everything and all that remains is a mess on the floor, I think of alternative sleeping arrangements.

I pull out two of the dresser drawers and lay them next to each other lengthwise, upside down. Then I lay the mat and old lab coats on top. I set everything I'll need tomorrow in the lavatory, so I won't waste time. I should be able to slide the mat next to the door in the morning easily now. When I'm lying on my new bed, thoughts keep me awake. I was able to help Charlie and I'm hoping I can help Viscerous, but all of this has interrupted my most important and genuine plan. Why did Cromwell need me? That question spun in my head as I fought sleep.

16
NIGHT

Vienna

"Changed your sleeping arrangements, I see," Colsam says, leaning to the side to view the contents of my room when he picks me up in the morning.

"I was ready for something new." I wonder if I should tell Colsam about my plan, that I understand how he wants to save his planet and is willing to isolate himself in this facility in order to do so.

"Seems like you have been a lot lately," he says, disheartened as he catches a glimpse of the mat next to the door.

"Plan on making a trip tonight?"

"Uh, maybe." I'd hoped he wouldn't see that.

"Be careful, Vienna, security continues to heighten. If you're caught, repercussions will be worse than usual."

"I will be. Thank you, Colsam."

He shakes his head and grunts as we zoom off to pick up Yesha.

"Morning, Colsam," Yesha says as she joins us.

"Morning," he responds.

"I can't believe they issued a lights-out. What are we, twelve-year-olds?"

"Security has been ordered to increase. There's not much we guards can do about it."

"You make any progress on your theory?" Yesha asks Colsam.

"Yeah, I've recruited enough that it should work."

"That is good news."

"In just over a week, we should be fully prepared."

"What are you two talking about?" I ask. "Aren't you afraid of putting people in danger?"

"Take a look around, Vienna," Colsam says. "They're already in danger."

"I still believe there's a better way."

"Oh, you think you can change Dr. Cromwell's mind," Yesha says. "Trust me, you can't. He has manipulated you, Vienna." Slowly, but with some force, Yesha is driving me to a point of complete frustration. I can't let her get to me. It's no wonder she's this extreme after losing her brother.

We arrive at the cafeteria. I'm furious with Yesha and Colsam. They're dismantling the process I'm trying to build though I haven't really been able to tell them my plan so it's not like I can blame them. At least I have over a week before their mutiny. The shuttle will be here before then. The pressure to get everything figured out in just days is suffocating. I sit with Quintus and Lucretia at their side of the table.

"Have you guys heard they're planning a revolution?"

"Yes, but I don't think we're really up to it," Lucretia responds. "We're still healing."

"Yes and I believe there's a safer route to be taken by everyone."

"Oh, what's that, Vienna?" Quintus leans forward full of interest.

"I'm going to get people on board the next shuttle."

"What, how?" Lucretia asks leaning forward now too in order to hear my whispering.

"Only a dozen or so people can fit on a shuttle, Vienna," Quintus adds.

"I know, I'm going to request a second," I say.

The looks of shock they give me make me queasy. They both lean back in their chairs.

"That's impossible," Quintus says.

"Not when you have something that Cromwell needs," I say and rise to put away my tray.

I sit back down at my usual side of the table with Quintus' and Lucretia's eyes following me the entire way.

"Finally decide to spend some time with me?" my dad asks as he gives me a side hug.

"What was that all about?" Al asks me.

"Oh, nothing." Yesha stares me down as I respond. Part of me wants to stick my tongue out at her like I did with Kitchen, but as my dad said, we're not playing games here.

When Yesha, Al, and my dad go to put away their trays, I approach Albina, "Will you help me get people on board the shuttle if I can promise Viscerous will be one of them?"

"Of course I'd do that, Vienna, but I don't see how you're going to be able to accomplish that. It's sweet of you to think of us though."

I exhale with her response. She too would not allow me to do what I plan on doing. "Just trust me, please."

"Okay."

At our lab, Al and I add the robotic bloodstream inhibitors to every non-bio body appointment schedule we can. Albina even helps us out. Positive move after positive move. I'm able to become more confident in my plan and map out the details.

I also pull up my study on the one live host rejection Cromwell hasn't figured out. I play around with my dad's idea. Using bloodstream bots, I test adaptation for live host acceptance similar to his anti-aging. I sprinkle in some of Yesha's technological information and realize the bots need the opposite of a firewall. They need a technological version of a party invitation.

That night I grab a roll from dinner and put it in my pocket. After Colsam drops off Yesha, who tells him goodbye, but not me, I decide I have to ask him a question even though I'm more than sure he won't like it.

"Colsam, if you were able to escape, would you?"

"Vienna, you know I want to stop what Cromwell's doing."

"Well then, if you were able to help others escape and then rid your planet of Cromwell completely, would you?"

"What? Well, yeah, but that's what the rebellion's for though. Which you seem to be against."

"You know we'll lose people in a revolution. Even if we win, many of your own kind will be killed."

"While that's true and would be difficult, Cromwell's treachery has to stop."

"What if I could make Cromwell quit voluntarily?"

"Vienna, that's impossible."

"Just wait, please, before you revolt. I'm begging you."

When Colsam drops me off, he doesn't say a word. He seems upset and distant with me. I wave goodbye, but he doesn't wave back. When he's turned away from me, I grab the mat and stop the door from shutting. With the mat's interference, it stops and lowers. My mat hangs partially out my door. I'm grateful for Al's information because when it's lights-out time, I won't be able to use the tablet to open the door.

I put on the clothes I wore here initially, minus the lab coat, thanks to my dream. When Al was picking the lock in my dream, he wore dark clothes to hide at night. Luckily, part of the adult outfit I stole from Mom's closet included a scarf. I tie it around my head. Then I rub my hands on the rock floor, thankful when they come up dirty. I apply dirt to all of my exposed skin, hoping the camouflage will work.

Before lights-out, I send Theopat a message. While email between employees here isn't allowed, I find that external email is. It can only reach people on this planet, so it's not like we could send a message home or anything. I ask Theopat if she and her brother would like to be aboard the next shuttle to Earth. She responds with an affirmative. I smile as I imagine her first day on Earth.

After that, I begin running the research on live hosts through my head. Most of my research has been on non-bio bodies, but I have also allowed myself to view some of Cromwell's other work during my lab research. I didn't tell anyone I was doing it and have tried my best to not even think about it, because this is a key piece to knowing what Cromwell needs.

Now as I allow myself to refocus on it, I remember the section on gut instinct pertaining to transplanted parts. Even though nature takes over, as Cromwell himself has told me, it takes time. The pure reflexes of a live host body continue. This is similar to the deflections of a non-bio body except they don't pose imminent danger. I sink further into the research. One of the live hosts found that he could cause the gut instinct to be stronger with repeated meditation prior to transplant. If that were to occur, it would negate my counter firewall bots.

When a couple hours have passed, I set the bread roll on the hill outside my quarters. Then I whistle just as Colsam did to tell Aviator when it was time to bring me back. I sit down and wait. The longer I wait, the more nervous I become. Finally, I decide to risk another whistle. At last, I hear the flapping of vulture wings when Aviator lands next to me. She eats the roll as I pet her. Adrenaline pumps through me as I hop on her back. We fly again. I'm becoming more comfortable with this form of transportation. I even hold my hands up in the air, trusting the bird completely as endorphins spread throughout my body. When we're above the medical facility and close to the other side, I ask the vulture a question as I did before.

My plan hinges on her reaction. If this doesn't work, my trip's going to be much longer, and I'm not sure I'll be able to return to my quarters in time.

"Can you land me on the roof, dear friend?"

I hold my breath, fearing she will shake her head side to side, but gulp air when she lowers toward the roof. She has to circle around to find a location free of solar panels. Once she does, we land, and I step off. I pet her to show my thanks. Without this vulture, I would be displaced on many levels far beyond my current physical one. This vulture has given me the freedom my spirit needed in order to not be crushed by the facility. I hug Aviator as I say goodbye. When the vulture flies off, I find myself missing her.

A whizzing sounds out, but the vulture dips, avoiding the fire from a club. A guard on the wall spotted the bird and must have disliked her landing on the roof. I drop to all fours and look back up to see the vulture has found safe harbor among the clouds. I have to focus on what I'm doing to override my fear of the guards. If they saw the vulture, did they see me?

The metal frame of a ladder circles over the edge of the roof. As I climb over and descend, I try to keep my body as flush to the dark building as I can. For some reason, the height seems to affect me more on the ladder than it did on the vulture. When I finally make it to the ground, I feel a little better until I realize my dark clothes were not the best choice. I'll stand out on the sand like a flashing sign. I know the sand won't stick to my clothes. It will just roll off. I attempt it anyhow. As I'm doing this, I notice how similar the sand is to the color of my skin and dread my following thought. I have to take my clothes off, wishing they could work like a chameleon instead.

Stripping off the pants and shirt is so invasive I begin to shake. Once I'm in only my undergarments, I sprint across to the shed faster than the pace of my heart. I'm thankful when I make it to the door unscathed except for a cut on my foot. I missed spotting a rock in the sand and ran right over it without the protection of shoes. The cut's not too deep though.

I try to stay as close to the sand as I can. I drop to my knees as I approach the shed door. At least the shed isn't as dark as the facility, but I still stand out a little. Luckily with the power still available on this side of the facility, I'm able to hack the lock. When I step inside, I'm surprised by how much is in there. It's like an inventory of every piece of equipment used in the facility, but I don't see what I need, tools that aren't used too often anymore. I believe, not that I have experience, I'll need a nail, hammer, a pry bar, and something like cardboard. It's going to take forever to find these things here.

I walk between shelves looking for anything unrelated to lab studies. I'm about to give up, figuring it may have been better to go to the garage, when I reach the furthest corner and see a toolbox. Yes, this is just what I need. I find the hammer and a nail and put them in, shoot! I don't have a pocket. I grab a tool belt on the shelf next to the toolbox. Now I'll really be stylish! A crowbar's on the shelf next to the tool belt. I have everything I need except for the cardboard. I'm going to have to return to my clothes before I go to Viscerous' door.

Sprinting again, my heart feels like it might explode out of my chest. I grab the pants because they are the thickest material and run to his door. The light at the corner of the building is close to the door. I'm afraid I might not be able to hide, but as I near, I see it falls short of the door I need.

On my knees again, I place a nail on the underside of a hinge. I've wrapped the nail with my pants, hoping to avoid the loud sound I could cause. Then I grab the hammer and begin tapping on the nail. As the hinge pin begins to rise, I hear a voice on the inside of the door. Thankfully, it's Viscerous.

"What's going on? Who's out there?"

I'm so glad I recognize the voice.

"Viscerous, it's me, Vienna. I'm getting you out of here."

"Vienna? How did you…? Oh never mind, you have to get out of here."

"No, they're planning worse punishment for you because I made a mistake during my trip to Planet Vortex. It's because of me the unscheduled shuttle came here and it's because of the shuttle your punishment will be worse."

"Forget about it, Vienna. Trust me, stopping the guard from burning Al wasn't the first counter move I've made. Plus, where would I go? They'd catch me if I ran. Also, I can't leave Albina behind."

I crumple to the ground. "We can work something out with Colsam. He has connections outside of the facility who could give you temporary safe harbor." I take a breath before continuing. "I can try to hack the security to Albina's quarters."

"I heard the power's off over there. And what if she was caught? Then she'd be punished too."

"Okay, but you can't protect her at all from in here."

"Vienna," Viscerous says. "Cog it all, you're right."

"I am? I mean, I am!"

"You seriously need to beef up your street smarts, kid."

I tap the other hinge pin out.

"Can you push the door out near the hinges, Viscerous?"

I'm elated when I feel the door move. Seeing his finger break free has me ecstatic. He sticks his head out looking in all directions and then steps out replacing the door.

"Um, you're missing a little something, Vienna." He points down.

I cover up the best I can with my arms. "Oh, yeah, how about you keep look out. Once I have the hinges back in place, we need to head to the ladder over there."

I place the pants on top of the hinge pin and hammer it back in place thankfully not feeling as though I'm hammering nails in a coffin lid. He's free!

"I need to return these tools. Can you meet me by the ladder?"

I run back to the shed and put the tools back in their place sans the nail because it could make a useful weapon. Sprinting back to the rest of my clothes, I hear voices around the corner of the facility.

Viscerous hands me my clothes and I put them on as quickly as I can. I motion for Viscerous to head up the ladder first. When we're twenty feet up on the ladder, two guards walk around the corner. One's the flame-throwing guard, and I don't recognize the other. We continue to climb as quietly and close to the building as we can, listening for any signs that we've been spotted the entire way.

"Looking forward to his punishment tomorrow," the flame-throwing guard says.

"Yeah, he's so big. He's about the only one of them that could actually put up a fight against us," says the other.

If they only knew of the fight they might be seeing. They walk toward Viscerous' door, surely to torture him with words about his impending punishment. Ha, ha, jokes on them but that means we don't have a lot of time.

When we get to the roof, I'm able to breathe because the guards didn't see us. I begin to whistle but stop myself. Aviator was almost harmed when she flew off the roof after transporting me here. I can't put another thing in danger. Plus, I'm not sure she could carry us both at the same time. Actually, Viscerous probably wouldn't go for that even if she could.

We run through the solar panels and multiple green glass pyramids. It takes much longer for us to run this zigzag pattern than it took the vulture to fly over. We spot a ladder on the other side and begin to descend. We head to my incubator, which is luckily close to the top of the hill.

We step inside my incubator. When I grab the mat to remove it, I hear a cough. I take a look in the direction it came from. Colsam's standing next to the red door. He shakes his head back and forth with a smirk on his face. Guess he caught my venture and saw that Viscerous is free.

I'm able to construct a hammock again with just the clothes so that Viscerous can have the mat and drawers for sleep.

"Thank you, Vienna."

"No, thank you. I thought you were going to argue with me forever."

"We still have some logistics to figure out, but I can do much more out here."

"I know you can, Viscerous."

"Good night."

"Night."

I'm assaulted with nightmares of all the things that have happened here when I fall asleep. The image of Quintus' flesh burned down to the muscle surfaces. And the whipping of Lucretia. Also, the battle of death for Rigled. I remember the way the blood flowed like a waterfall. The thought of Marcus reminds me of the boogey man I'd feared as a child. As dawn breaks, it hits me. We're going to have to take on the man himself, Cromwell.

There's no room for error.

17
TIME DILATION

Al

I can't get the army of guards approaching us out of my head. It felt like they took a rib when they fully cuffed Viscerous. Not again. I cannot lose him too. Colsam was right. He didn't ruin the study. This is absolute bullshit. Of course, he's probably taunting guards from his cell right now. A smile breaks through at the thought of this.

"It's about time you showed up. This place is in shambles you know," Yesha says interrupting my thoughts.

"My bad, I had a project to attend to," I reply.

I had to get Albina, Septimus, Yesha, Colsam, and Theopat together. I hope Albina's head is clear despite Viscerous being imprisoned. They're always glued to each other. It's got to be hard for her, but I need her clear-cut logic. The revolution has to happen now. I just wish Sierra would join us. She's the missing piece. She's been the missing piece all along.

"Oh boy, a project," Yesha continues.

"Cut it out, you two. Time's limited," Albina says. That's Albina. Even with everything she's going through, she's the one holding us together.

I hope we can organize something so well thought out, so undeniably true that Sierra can't refuse. She'll be forced to join and let go of her ridiculous notion.

"That's right! We're getting closer in numbers. Theopat's had some luck," Colsam adds.

"What about timing?" Yesha asks.

"The guards have doubled. They're watching our every move. Are you guys sure about this?" Septimus asks.

"We're going to use it to our advantage," Albina says.

"How?" Septimus asks.

"The schedule falls so that our ally guards are together in a few days. There will be direct access. We can contain the enemy without damage, and we can escape." I say.

"Also, I've made some headway on Vienna's idea," Albina says.

"Oh?" I ask.

"Yeah, I think I'm headed in the right direction to find a way to neutralize the guards' weapons so that we can minimize the casualties on all sides. It's definitely not fool proof."

"Really? Can we make sure the weapons work if they're pointed in Cromwell's direction?" Yesha asks.

I roll my eyes at her and she gives me a 'what' shrug.

"Let me focus on the problems I already have before you add to them. I was able to develop a magnet to throw off the chain whips, but I would like to find a way to test it. It's been more difficult to find ways to extinguish the flame throwing clubs. I'm currently experimenting with neon gas."

"How have you gotten away with that during heightened security?" Colsam asks.

"Well, not all of the guards have been trained in the

sciences so I was able to claim the activity was for authorized testing."

Now Colsam's rolling his eyes at her until Septimus interrupts.

"That's all very good but have you thought about the World Government?" Septimus asks.

"Don't worry about that. I've got it under control. Long overdue, trust me," I say.

"I think I see why you and my daughter get along so well."

"About that... she's still not fully on board..."

"I'm worried for her. She's too close to Cromwell."

"I know. I'll talk to her."

"Good, I'm afraid she won't listen to me."

"Does she listen to anyone?" I ask with a wink.

———

I know it's risky because of what happened last time but it's back to the tunnels for me and this time the plan is to take it a step further to find out what Cromwell's plans are for Sierra.

This will be the last time I'm surrounded by the watermelon smell. I know everyone's scheduled to be in the cafeteria, but this isn't the first time I've played hooky. It was more difficult with the constant monitoring, but I scored a few talents from a misspent youth.

Opening the vent from the tunnel to Cromwell's study is something new to me. I stick the mirror out first to ensure I'm alone, which I am. There's actually less screws on this one...kind of surprising given Cromwell's normal paranoid style. The pictures I've seen from the tunnels are all still here. I go to the piece of furniture that's always grabbed my attention in this room.

The place where he sits, where I've imagined him scheming his evil plans; his desk. I reach for the lower right drawer. This is where the answers will be. This is the key. I pull on the handle…nothing. It doesn't budge.

That's when I see it, the holograph combination lock. Shit! I hit my forehead with my hand. I sit in his cringeworthy chair staring at the walls in frustration. Those same pictures on the walls stare back at me. Sorna and Damien; what were their birthdays? I try them in the lock, no luck. It dawns on me… the day they were lost…Cha Ching…access granted.

I open the drawer relieved and freaked out at the same time. What will I find? The first file is it, her name and picture right there in front of me. I breath in and open it…and I'm unable to breathe again for the next thirty seconds. This is worse, it's impossible. He's never gone this far before.

———

"I can't get around the spindle proteins," I say.

"You don't have time to allow for the growth required with that procedure anyway," Albina says.

"What if we could greatly expedite the growth process?"

"You'd still have to figure out a way to prevent the dyes and ultraviolet light from damaging the cell and preventing growth."

"Shit, you're right!"

I rake my hands through my hair. How am I going to save her? The rebellion's the only way. It's always been the only way. Why am I wasting my time trying to clone her?

"Calm down and just wait a minute. Don't be a hothead. Let's think this through. What about Microtubule nucleation?" Albina snaps me out of it.

"Yeah and combine it with Microtubule transport. I think you're onto something there."

Maybe, just maybe we can save her.

18
TEST

Vienna

"HAVE A NICE EXCURSION LAST NIGHT?" COLSAM ASKS with his usual playfulness, but then his face turns serious. "Vienna, you can't just roam about like that."

"I know," I sigh, still a little hazy with delirium. "I was able to free Viscerous. Can you get him and Albina to Theopat or somewhere safe away from the facility?"

"Yeah," Colsam says. "We should be able to get something worked out."

"Great, actually I built a ladder over the wall that might help."

"You did what?"

"Thank you, Colsam. Where are we headed?"

"Oh, I'm to take you to the adjacent cliff again."

"What? Wait, before I forget, I promised Viscerous I'd tell you something."

"What's that?"

"You have to promise it won't expedite the revolution."

"Unfortunately, there's no way I can speed things up. What is it?"

"Viscerous found out the name of Cromwell's lawyer. It's Hydor Lilton."

Colsam's face scrunches up in a way I've never seen before. "I see. Thank you for telling me."

We pick up Yesha, who gives me the "I told you so" look.

Everyone's forced to assemble at the arena where Rigled was killed, like ants to an anthill for what was planned to be Viscerous' punishment. I don't know why we're here. Everyone skitters to their seats, afraid to approach the arena. I find Albina and sit next to her, immediately holding her hand.

"Albina, Viscerous is in my quarters. Colsam and I are going to find safe harbor for you two outside of the facility."

She hugs me.

Al's talking to Yesha; a glare crosses my face. He gives her a disappointed look and then heads in our direction. He sits down on the other side of Albina and grabs her opposite hand.

"I'm sorry, Albina. I wish we could revolt right now."

"That's okay, Al. Vienna has Viscerous in her quarters," Albina whispers.

That's when it happens. My dad is escorted into the viewing area in place of Viscerous, my heart pounds so hard I can hear the beat in my ears. He's on display like a circus act, only no archaic clowns flit about for comical relief. Dad is strapped to an upright gurney. The tension within the audience of subjects and doctors is almost visible, a purple cloud above our heads. The seating's uncomfortable, but no one pays that any mind. All eyes are glued to the viewing area. I hold my breath and make a wish for my dad:

Please let Dr. Cromwell have a particle of sympathy.

Don't let him continue his path of soul-crushing torture.

As I lift my head, I know my wishes aren't going to come

true today. An employee rolls out a huge, clear tank full of water. Then Cromwell speaks.

"Facility members, this man attempted to plan a revolution. That is not allowed."

Al's free hand balls up into a fist before he switches places with Albina.

The guard closest to my dad attaches a huge chain hanging from a crane to Dad's gurney. Dad signs *always and forever* to me. As the chain begins to lift Dad, Al begins to stand, but Septimus looks at him and shakes his head. Al sits with a crushed spirit.

I...*can't...breathe*! Of all the things I had been worried about, this was not one of them. Dad's been replaced. Cromwell doesn't care about him.

The crane lowers him into the water and my dad holds his breath. Watching him like that for seconds and minutes is absolute torture.

I stand up not even fully realizing what I'm doing. "Cromwell, I will kill myself if you do this." I raise my arm up holding the sharp tip of the nail I saved against my skin with my opposite hand. "That vital testing you need will have to be delayed...indefinitely."

Al grabs me but doesn't pull on my arm or push the nail away. Instead he turns away to block any oncoming guards.

Cromwell's eyes flicker. He looks down and, for the first time, I see him make an uncalculated move. He pulls on the cuffs of his shirtsleeves. A small move that most wouldn't even notice, but I know that it means I got under his skin. Cromwell looks at me. Dad doesn't have a lot of time and Cromwell still hasn't answered.

"Stop," he orders. "Pull him out of the tank."

The guards begin lifting the gurney, but Dad's hanging on by a thread.

"If we save him, you will be taken right away," Cromwell says to me.

"That's fine, but you're losing time."

Dad stops breathing and his eyes roll back. A pain squeezes my chest, tightening my lungs.

"Get the cardiopulmonary resuscitation bots," Cromwell orders.

A guard pulls up the holograph and navigates to a timed chest compressor. They place it on Dad's chest. The screen depicts a countdown. Three, two, one, clear and the screen turns red. Dad's body jolts on the upright gurney. Nothing, he doesn't move, and the monitor read shows a flat line.

"Again," Cromwell yells.

Artificial ventilation is then administered. When his body moves this time, Dad's sharp intake of air causes everyone in the audience to rise and clap. Al stays with me and grabs my hand holding me back. Nurses have moved to the area to assist in Dad's recovery. Yesha heads that way to join and help them. As much as I've been mad at her I'm grateful for her now. She will look after him. She looks at me and nods her head.

I'm frozen. Everything's backward. I should be down there with him. Cromwell nods his head to the side and a guard runs up and removes the nail from my grip. It's Cromwell's smile that breaks my trance.

"No! Cromwell, you can't take her," Al says.

"She gave her word," Cromwell says with a vile breath.

Then, he nods his head at the guards again. It's weird. It's as if they know exactly what he means with that simple nod. But, they couldn't have known to expect this. Cromwell and more guards head in our direction. I believe Cromwell's grinding his teeth, furious. When he approaches, Al stands between us.

"Your presence is not needed," Cromwell tells Al.

Al stays put. Cromwell tilts his head and a guard steps in front of him.

"It's okay, Al." I replace his spot in front of the guard and look him in the eye. "I'll be all right."

Cromwell sets his hand firmly on my shoulder as he guides me away. I cringe at his touch. I take one last look at Dad before we leave. He raises his hand ever so slightly. Yesha gives me a thumbs up letting me know he'll be okay.

I'm put in electric handcuffs as soon as we exit the area. That's when I notice their shock capability. My heart darkens a little with the touch of metal on my wrists. While I've felt psychologically bound, this is the first time I've physically been in cuffs. Colsam isn't the one to transport me on the railcar this time. Instead, it's a guard I don't even recognize. Do they grow them here or something? My heart pounds deeper into my chest as we approach the facility. Cromwell and the guards are silent as we move through the cafeteria and into the hall. When we reach Cromwell's hall, I find myself no longer interested in the holograph walls. When we stop, Cromwell orders the guard to remove my handcuffs and leave. I'm a little surprised he's doing this with the move I just made.

"I know you only acted for care of your friend, Vienna, but do you understand what kind of behavior this could lead to?"

"Yes, but I couldn't watch him be harmed and sit back doing nothing."

"I know. I was expecting your group to do exactly what you did. I needed a reason to not kill. With the talk of mutiny going on an act of kindness was necessary, but I couldn't let people think I had gone soft."

"What?" I take a breath before continuing hoping to turn the direction of this conversation. "I found the key to fix live host rejection. The one you haven't found."

Cromwell's face changes completely as I talk. He's

weighing alternatives in his head. I can visually see when it clicks. Then his face unexpectedly shifts back to a relaxed expression.

"Don't worry about it. Have a seat. Do you need some time to clear your head?" he asks as he begins pulling up the screens.

He doesn't even want to discuss the anti-rejection development. He's just worried about testing me. I am so confused.

"Ah, no, I'm fine."

Even though his demeanor has returned to the calm one I'm used to here, he still uses enough force when placing probes on me to move my head. We run through the test again. There are new questions, but the forms that had caused fuzziness in my brain before are now clear. I would like to slow the test, but part of the result depends on time. When the result shows on the screen, I smile because Cromwell seems elated and then shocked by the results. I remember Albina telling me not to allow his words to affect me. Cromwell rips the probes from my head, even tearing a few strands of hair from my scalp. Then he puts the case with vials and needles on the table. A nurse rolls a bed in too. It feels like spiders are crawling up and down my skin.

"Please take a seat on the bed."

I stand up and head that way, trying to walk as slow as I can. The feeling that I'm walking on pins and needles has returned. The fear of the pain I'm about to feel is like those nail points gouging me with each step, as tingles spread from my feet to my head. When I sit on the bed, I half expect there to be leather straps to bind me down, but I don't see any.

"Vienna, we are going to draw blood to double check a few things. I'm sure you've had that done before," Cromwell says as he rolls the results holograph over to the bed. He doesn't face it my direction this time and with the protector on the backside, I'm unable to see the screen. He takes one of the hairs that had ripped from my scalp and places it in a box. He presses a button, and I can hear clicks. As he faces the screen, I notice a reflection on one of the framed pictures about the room. I can only see the top half of the holograph screen, but that's better than none. DNA results pull up. I see the expected double X on one side of the screen, but on the other I see an XY. That's not mine.

The nurse begins to wipe my arm with an alcohol swab. Luckily, I'm looking at her when Cromwell turns my way. I want to look back at the multidimensional prism photo, but I can't let him catch me. If the side with the Y chromosome isn't mine, whose could it be? When I peek back, I see more chromosome bars. They're not identical, but I see the same words pop up with every chromosome— "biological similarities."

When the needle enters my arm and blood's drawn, Cromwell uses a dropper to put some of my blood into the box. I see my side of the screen light up to note that a few of the findings with the hair sample were inaccurate.

Cromwell taps the screen a few times, and I can see "biological similarities" popping up again. I have to scratch my head once when he looks at me before I can deflect my eyes from looking at the photo so he can't see what I'm doing. He adjusts the holograph, and I've lost my view. The nurse reaches to my abdomen and pulls up my shirt.

"What are you doing?" I ask.

"She needs to lower your pants so we can access your hip," Cromwell says.

"Why do you need to access my hip?"

"We're going to run a bone marrow biopsy."

This I had never expected.

"Don't worry, I know you don't respond to anesthesia. We have a couple alternatives. There's one that will put you into a lighter sleep but tends to work on those whose bodies refuse traditional anesthesia, or we can use enough local numbing that you will feel less pain."

"The local," I respond without hesitation. There's no way I want to be knocked out around this man. How does he know I don't respond to anesthesia?

After that, the nurse continues to lift my shirt and unbutton my pants. I swipe her hand away.

"I can do it." I unzip my pants, roll them down just far enough to reveal my hips, and lay on my stomach.

Cold spreads across my skin as an alcohol swab wipes and then Betadine is rubbed all over my skin to prevent infection. I feel the needle prick through my skin for the local, but after that there's less pain than I expected. I feel tension as the scalpel enters my skin. There is a burning and throbbing sensation. Then one of the worst sounds I can imagine begins. The laser drill enters my hip. The pressure intensifies as the bone within the drill's diameter is crushed. Even with the local my hands shake from the pain. I'll have nightmares of that sound forever. Once I'm sutured, the tests are complete. The nurse helps me sit up and put my clothes back in place. While she's doing this, the screen appears on a different multidimensional prism photo. In big, green letters are the words CANDIDATE MATCH.

Cromwell and the nurse leave, allowing me to get my bearings. There are ten vials of blood on the table next to me. I hadn't noticed that many had been taken. Moving off the bed is difficult. My hip aches when I move my legs. Instead, I adjust the bed to a half upright position, lying on the side opposite the hip in pain. Counting to ten doesn't help me relax. I feel nervy and on edge. I look around at all of the photos. Damien smiles at me mischievously from one. That's when it hits me. Cromwell isn't looking for a good artery transplant, limb transplant, or even brain matter transplant this time. He's looking for the live host he's been waiting for.

He wants to implant that snotty, little kid's conscience and memory into me, the candidate match. I have to get out of here.

Using my arms helps lift me from the bed and keep the weight off the bad hip. Walking feels strange, as if there's a missing piece in my body. I take light, quick steps on that side allowing my good side to bear most of the weight. Cromwell enters when I'm just a few more steps from the door.

"Up and walking already?" he asks. "Glad to see you have good recovery skills."

I bet you're glad my body's able to recover quickly—your son will need it.

"You are free to go, but don't think about escaping the facility. You care for many here, and I will target them the second you leave."

"That may be true, but I know you need me to be out there with them. You're walking a fine line with a revolution that's very likely to happen. If I disappear, that coup will be on your front doorstep in a heartbeat."

Cromwell cracks the vertebrae on his neck in an overpowering manner.

When I finally make it past the holograph walls, I'm able to breathe. His family must still be at the satellite hotel otherwise he would have never let me go. I still have some power left. I have to lean against the wall to catch my breath.

Since Cromwell used the advantage I had over him, the retest, in exchange for saving my dad, I'm going to have to work with what I have left. After seeing the results, I know what that means for me. But he *is* going to need the anti-rejection information. I can feel the pain worsen. The local must be wearing off. As I limp toward the cafeteria, a scientist I don't recognize passes by.

"Could you please tell me what time it is?"

He looks at his watch. "Five minutes until dinner."

"Thank you." I didn't realize that much time had passed. Good thing I still have five minutes. It's going to take me that long to get down the last section of the hallway with my limp.

When I finally make it into the cafeteria, Al spots me first. He notices my limp. "Are you okay? What happened?"

"I'll be fine. I don't really want to talk about it. Could you please help me with my tray?"

He picks one up and begins piling it with every food and drink available. As we're walking to our table, Yesha sees me. She runs to me and puts my arm on the bad side over her shoulders, acting as my crutch. She helps me sit down, and Al sits on my other side. Everyone stares at me.

"I'm fine, please eat," I say, uncomfortable with the stares.

"I'm sorry I've been such a bitch lately," Yesha says.

"You're just trying to rectify what happened, Yesha. I get it." She actually smiles at my response. Too bad we can't spend time together like old times, even though those had been digital. I miss the simple breaking of rules to save koalas and things like that.

"How's my dad?"

"He's recovering. He's going to be all right."

I nod holding back tears as she gives me a side hug.

Albina stretches out her arm out to give me a hug too. I hold her there for a second longer as I whisper, "Can you make sure the shuttle leaves on time?" I hesitate for a second, "Whether I'm on board or not."

"You have my word," she whispers back. She rises and brushes her shirt, straightening the wrinkles. She smiles the smile a parent gives an unknowing child at me before leaving to hopefully join Viscerous. There are no tears in her eyes, but they're puffy.

Al hugs me and then holds my hand, not releasing it. "You're a hero, Sierra!" He smiles, and I'm glad to not see a tear in his eye.

If only my dad could hug me. Tears sting my eyes, but I stop them from spilling out.

Al continues to hold my hand the entire meal, feeding me the whole time, so I don't have to use my other hand.

Other people keep approaching and giving me a nod of approval. Many of these people I've never met, but they speak to me as if we've known each other my entire time here.

When Lucretia and Quintus approach, I see that their wounds are completely healed. The scars on them both are validation for my actions.

"What you did for your dad today was amazing, Vienna," Quintus says.

Lucretia gives me a hug, and I remind her too, "Don't forget the shuttle."

After the meal, Yesha and Al both help me to the red door. I hold on a little longer than I have before. This is a comfort I've yearned for lately. I wish I could bottle it up and take it everywhere with me. When it's Al's turn, we hug and he peck-kisses me. The butterflies have become angels. I let the feeling lift me from my physically depressed state. I smile and blow him a kiss as his railcar leaves.

I limp as I step forward with the line and with less help. Yesha notices my limp and switches sides to put my bad side arm over her shoulders again. She makes a perfect-sized crutch. I smile sideways at her, and she smiles in return. When we're first in line and Colsam sees us, he steps off the car, walks to me, and lifts me up. He carries me to the car, but before setting me down he asks me a question.

"What's the best position for you? What hurts?"

"Um, my hip. Can I sit sideways so I can lean on my good one?"

"Of course." He gently sets me down sideways.

Yesha boards behind me and puts one arm around me, the

other holding onto the bar. Funny that in the beginning I didn't want this seat, and now I'm grateful for it.

We drop off Yesha, who hugs me for the first time. "Colsam, I was holding her steady with one hand. Do you think you can drive with one hand and hold her with the other?" Yesha says before stepping off the railcar.

"Of course."

She holds up the "I love you" sign language symbol that my dad did in the first days behind her frosted glass. In fact, many incubators we pass have the same symbol. It's hard to keep the tears from spilling out.

When we reach my incubator, Colsam puts the car in park. He turns around and picks me up. When he carries me in and sets me down on the bed Viscerous used in a position so that my bad hip's up, he clears his throat as if there's a frog in it. He kneels down beside me and brushes the hair out of my face.

"Do you need help with pajamas or to the lavatory?"

"No, I can manage. Hey, Colsam," I say.

"Yes, Vienna?"

"Remember the scenario of Cromwell voluntarily letting people go that I mentioned?"

"Don't do it, Vienna. Whatever it is that you're planning, please don't do it."

"Promise me that you'll see to it that Cromwell follows through."

"There's no way I can stop you, is there?" His hands softly fist in my hair as he leans down and kisses me on the top of my head. He begins to walk toward the door. "I promise, with all of my heart."

Before Colsam can leave, Albina and Viscerous exit the lavatory that I hadn't realized two people could fit in!

"Colsam, were you able to find a way to sneak these two out?"

"Yes, but we must act quickly but not right now. We need to wait until the coast is clear."

Finding a spot for three people in my incubator proves difficult after Colsam leaves to finish taking everyone to their quarters. Albina and Viscerous settle with leaning against the back wall. That way their shadows won't be seen by others either.

There's an awkwardness in the close quarters while we wait. Viscerous shows Albina my hammock and they discuss how one should be in every incubator. The way they debate over the best approach to go about this reminds me of what I think my mom and dad would have been like had they not been separated over the years. They're in tune with one another and, while some on the outside might think they were bickering, I can see the mutual admiration they have for each other. Then they turn to me.

"I heard you were pretty ballsy out there, kid," Viscerous breaks the silence.

"Yeah, she was," Albina adds.

"It's what I get for hanging out with people like you." I smirk despite everything.

"But for real, are you okay?" Viscerous asks.

"Yeah, what did he do to you? Why are you limping so bad?"

"It's nothing to worry about."

And Colsam re-enters the incubator in the nick of time.

When they leave, and I'm alone, tiredness fully sets in. I've pushed my body far beyond its limit. As I close my eyes, I swear death is staring me in the face, and she's smiling, calling me her way. I think of all the people I'm about to emancipate, and I smile back.

19
TEAM

Vienna

THE NEXT DAY, I FEEL A HUNDRED TIMES BETTER. MY HIP feels normal, and my energy has increased. When I look out, the light's brighter than usual. I feel free of the almost shattering of my resolve yesterday. I look at the sun and realize it's almost lunchtime. Did I sleep through the alarm? I slowly get up, testing my strength, and head to the shower. When I step out, I feel like a brand-new person. I put on my clothes thankfully before the door opens. It's Colsam.

"You feeling up to another day?"

"Um, yeah, how was I able to sleep in?"

"Cromwell told the guards to let you."

"Really?"

"Yeah, hop on board. Your dad gave them your Mom's vegan meatloaf recipe, and they're serving it in the cafeteria now." Maybe Cromwell does have a particle of sympathy, gifting me a last meal.

"Dad's better! Cromwell breaking his rules…this is unheard of." I jump on the railcar. Instead of holding the bar, I hug Colsam from behind the entire way. I can see his cheeks expand behind his head yet again. He's smiling.

As we meet the red door, we're in the midst of silence. Looking out at the desert with beach like sand, I think about how I've always been with a group here. Is that part of how Cromwell has successfully hidden things? When unobserved, we're usually alone, unable to communicate. When together, we're watched. A few people in the cafeteria clap as I walk in and it fills me with the stamina I need. I smile and wave back. Al walks up to me and begins to put my arm around his shoulders.

"I'm fine now. I can walk."

He holds my hand instead.

I turn around and look at Colsam. "Thank you!"

Eating my mom's meatloaf recipe is like nothing I've been served here before. I actually ask for seconds. I think back to her twirling her hair before I left. The years we've been together, and now it feels as if we've been apart for years, though it's been nowhere near that long.

I wonder if Dad feels like he's been gone for more than a decade. I imagine them seeing each other again after all of these years, embracing each other. I imagine Vex rolling up and delivering a meal they can share together that has been prepared by Kitchen. Everyone seems more chipper with my recovery, but before too long we are told to go to our assigned labs again.

It's good to be back in the lab. Al approaches the wall of tallies with the Airblow, his veins protruding beneath the skin on his neck and forehead. I can see the muscles ripple through his back as he begins scrawling ferociously. *This must end!* I take the Airblow from his hands and approach the wall to add *Now!* It's like his anger and strength have seeped into my bones, but I feel the pull from within; this is of my own making, a fight that's been brewing for years.

When I return and set down the Airblow, he lifts my chin with his hand, and I grab his hair at the nape of his neck. When I kiss him it feels like the walls around this place have crumbled. It's like I can soar with this sensation. I no longer feel desperate or afraid of this place. All of a sudden, I'm filled with a strength I never knew existed. When he pulls away, I see one of the brightest smiles I've ever seen on anyone's face.

Guards enter the lab. "We are here for assigned lab observation."

Cromwell enters behind the guards. Al picks up the Airblow and points it at Cromwell's face. The guards lift their flame-throwing clubs and chain whips, readying them in Al's direction. I step in front of Al and wrap my body around him the best I can.

"I need a negotiation before I can give you what you want, Cromwell."

He tilts his head away from the direction of the Airblow to look at me. "Drop your weapons," he orders the guards.

I step in front of the Airblow, pushing Cromwell back. "Al, if you care for me please lower the Airblow." I want to protect him, but I'm sure Cromwell has witnessed our growing close and just saw me attempt to turn into a soft pretzel shield around Al's body. I don't know if I'll have another chance to tell him how much I care.

He reluctantly lowers the Airblow and looks down. The tear that rolls off his cheek sends stabbing pain through my heart. "I love you, Al. Thank you for my first kiss."

He grabs the back of my neck and kisses me again, sending my heart into what feels like palpitations, before Cromwell grabs my arm, yanking me back.

"I love you too," Al breathes out.

The guards follow Cromwell with me in his grip. I soon

find myself walking down the same damn holographic hallway.

"I know what you need, Cromwell."

"Yeah and what's that?"

"I'm the perfect match as a host body for your son, Damien."

"You catch on quick," he sarcastically replies.

"But, you haven't figured out all anti-rejection processes. There's one missing. Also, did you know that pure reflexes of a live host body continue after implantation?"

"What makes you think one of my scientists haven't figured out the anti-rejection? And, I could have ways to intervene pure reflexes."

"You wouldn't have released Septimus if you did."

I catch the slight contraction of his forehead and the muscles of his left cheek. No, he doesn't have the answer.

I continue, "I've figured it out, but need certain demands to be met before I'll be willing to share. Also, did you know that the reflexes can grow with meditation from the host prior to implantation? I've done preliminary meditation but can continue and make them grow even further beyond your control."

"What negotiations were you speaking of earlier?"

"I would like certain individuals to be sent to Earth on tomorrow's shuttle. I'd also like a second shuttle."

"I can't do that."

"Don't mess with me. Yes, you can. What about the emergency pod that remained from the unscheduled shuttle? And, how was it that Dr. Bargory was on board that shuttle? I also want the current processes here to end. You'll have no need for them once the procedure's complete."

"How are you going to change the activities after the procedure?" he asks, thinking he's caught a weakness and that my meditation practice will be incapable of growing once Damien's conscience and memory are in my body.

"Meditation can become contingent upon certain events if done right," I answer looking him straight in the eyes.

He actually drops his jaw with this response.

"So you want me to free those interested in no longer being at the facility and cease current procedures for those who stay. Where will that leave me and Damien with the government?"

I'm caught in a moment of surprise, but it only takes one gulp to regroup. "You're able to go to many other planets than this one and the people staying here will only be interested in returning Planet Vortex to what it once was. I just need at least twelve hours of time."

I know I'm leaving other planets at his mercy, but right now I really just need him to buy into my offer because twelve hours might just be long enough for a revolt. I should have worked with my friends long ago.

He marches back and forth in the room before returning to me. "Deal, but if you fall short on your side. I will kill more."

I take a deep breath in and continue to stare directly in his eyes. "Deal." I extend my hand for a shake. He does the same. I grip his hand to answer his strength and find that my own matches his.

"Meet me in the hallway opposite the labs. From the front entrance, you'll turn the opposite direction as you did when you first got here. There'll be three doors. Meet at the middle one," he calls after me as I leave.

He doesn't know just how familiar I am with that door. Well, the door on the other side of the room. Ironic that it's the same cell Viscerous and Quintus were held in. As I walk into the cafeteria for dinner, I approach Lucretia and Quintus first. "I have reserved seats for you on board tomorrow's shuttle."

"Really?" Quintus asks.

I point to the podium and their eyes follow my finger. When they look at the podium, Cromwell nods his head their way in approval. I'm sure Cromwell will believe everything's going according to his plans while witnessing my activity.

I go to Yesha. "I have Cromwell's word that processes will end here. He is going to step down."

She looks at Cromwell, who gives her the same nod of approval.

"It comes on one condition."

"What's that?" she asks.

"Make sure Pixie's on board tomorrow's shuttle."

"You have my word."

Then I do the hardest thing for me to do. I sit between my dad and Al. "We have reserved spots on tomorrow's shuttle. Can you believe it, we're going back home!"

My dad speaks first, "What? How did you do that?"

"Thanks to Mom's research, I found a key piece in Cromwell's studies but won't give it to him until we've lifted off. Just take a look at him." I point in Cromwell's direction again, and he nods his compliance.

"Wow, Sierra! You're amazing. You're smarter than I ever have been."

I hug my dad glad he bought the story. I feel absolutely remorseful about lying to him. Here we've just been able to see each other again and within no time at all, I'm breaking his trust.

Shortly after that, my dad and Al speak in unison, "What about the procedures here?"

"He's going to end those and leave Planet Vortex. Colsam and Yesha will be in charge of that."

When they look in Yesha's direction, she gives them a nod of affirmation too.

They both squeeze my hands, but Al tilts his head sideways. He knows something's going on.

We eat, well, they eat. I push my food around, taking a few bites here and there, but only so that I don't raise any flags. When we line up at the red door, Al's hand doesn't leave mine. As soon as my dad has boarded his railcar, Al speaks, "What's going on, Sierra? Things can't be as easy as you're making them sound."

"But they are. I found how live hosts could monopolize the gut reaction even after implantation, causing the issues like deflection in non-bio bodies. And, I found a reverse firewall procedure for the anti-rejection bots." It probably shouldn't feel so natural to falsely keep up pretenses.

"He bought into that? Why were you so debilitated after the testing?"

"I offered myself up as a test subject. He inserted foreign cells into my hip to study the results. That's why I was limping." I hate lying like this, but I need everyone to buy in, otherwise the sacrifice will not be worth it. But Al and I's relationship is so fresh. It's grown rapidly due to the constant fear we've been living in. I'm sure at home we'd be able to let it simmer and get to know one another more. Instead, we're doing the opposite.

"Well, thank you for doing that," Al says as he kisses me. Heat rushes through my lips to behind my eyelids. My legs begin to wobble beneath me, but he holds me up. I trace the line of his jaw and then move to his collarbone with my finger. Then it's his time to board the railcar.

When Yesha and I board our railcar, I speak with Colsam, "Cromwell has agreed to allow those who want to return home to be aboard tomorrow's shuttle. He's also agreed to end processes here, but I need your help with that."

"Really?" Colsam asks.

"Yeah, Dr. Cromwell even nodded in approval," Yesha adds.

"Okay," he says.

"You and Yesha will be in charge of overseeing new processes," I say.

"Sounds good," Colsam says.

We drop off Yesha and then Colsam speaks to me, "What did you give up in order to achieve this?"

"Don't worry about it, Colsam."

"But I do. I care for you, Vienna."

"I care for you too, but if you really care for me, you'll be sure processes end."

"All right." He hugs me before I return to my quarters.

I feel dizzy with every emotion that's been pulled through me. I brush my teeth in front of the mirror, feeling like the same girl who did this at home, but also like a grown woman who has looked at her face in the mirror too many times. I put on the pajamas, thinking of the billions of people who have done this before me. I'm really just a blip on the map. At a certain point, the mundanity of everything overwhelms me, and I decide it's best to go to sleep.

As I stare out into the sky with multiple moons, I spot a vulture flying in circles above me. My muscles have memorized the flights we've had. It's my vulture, and she's waiting for a whistle that might never come. Then a gas drifts through the intercom. It's an anesthesia that I don't respond to. Fifteen minutes after this, a guard enters my incubator. He's wearing the tool belt I had just a few nights ago; it's all such a blur that I can't even remember the number of days it's been. The thought of me racing across the sand in my skivvies makes me want to laugh, but I'm too engrossed in following the guard's movements. Cromwell knows I don't respond to anesthesia. Isn't this risky?

He removes the intercom face and places a camera within. I look out and see guards entering and leaving multiple incubators. Guess Cromwell wants to be sure none of us escape or revolt before he gets what he wants. I begin the meditation I've been participating in for a long time, but this time I change it. The mantra going through my head is one of acceptance only if certain measures are followed. I'm glad Cromwell can view my meditation on camera. After the mantra, I try to fall asleep, as if that were possible.

I run through memories in my head. Al's kiss and the reverberating song in my heart. Lucretia's and Quintus' love for one another even in this dismal place. Albina's and Viscerous' not only love for each other, but the parenting love they've given Al over the past few years. Yesha's strength and feistiness in honor of her loved one. How much she and I have detested each other and cared for one other at the same time. Colsam's befriending of me, an alien. My study with Dad, milk curds smelling vile while we were finally able to enjoy each other's company.

All of these memories and moments could have never been mine if my dad were not an interplanetary medical genius and our vacations had been on ocean beaches. Since I can't sleep, I get up and pack Mom's purse with enough things to look sufficient. I use steam from the shower to unwrinkle one of Dad's old lab coats. Screw the rules, I'm wearing his coat tomorrow. I realize I never tested the Science Olympiad pill during my time here. I put extra clothes in the purse and will add the toiletry bag to the purse tomorrow.

Then I lie down, knowing I only have a couple hours until the alarm. As I drift off, a song my mom used to sing enters my mind. The song's different, like an older version, slow and deep almost like an enchanting, good witch putting you into a trance.

(Back to the dream of a hundred plus years ago.)
Oh once there was a little girl whose
tears dripped into ponds of sorrow.
All would circle and sing gathering waves
pooling together non-bias.

Follow all couples, for it is the way
promises and vows soon let down.
But what's in the heart foreshadows
when love conquers all enemies.

Oh once there was a ceremony that
bound one another forever.
Only a half of these were to remain
taking them away for always.

Be quiet you don't want them to hear you
for secrets prove misadventure.
And all still circled the pond that had pooled
in only heartbreak and gallows.

Whatever's trying to get a message through to me, it's loud and clear, like I should be able to conquer the enemy.

I'm riddled with questions and completely uneasy as I head to breakfast the next morning with the purse on my shoulder.

As soon as everyone's finished their breakfast, Cromwell makes an announcement.

"Everyone, apart from the following people I call, need to head to their labs. The remaining people are to set out on an offsite mission."

As he begins calling the names of the people I care for, my heart starts pounding in excitement. He's been watching me closer than I realized. He even calls people I didn't think he knew I cared for. As the list of people increases, I begin doing the math of who can fit on board. Before he leaves, he shakes his head to the side and nods to me. I know this is my cue. How did he know I needed to keep it a secret? I don't have time to figure him out. I head to the exit to stick with my cover.

As everyone else approaches with their belongings, suits, and pouches—apparently my statements last night had been strong enough—I wait for all of them to gather and exit the red door. I want to touch them all, but physical contact is powerful and I'm afraid of what they might see. I smile at the sweet woman who gave me Rigled's card as she passes to exit out the red door too.

My dad stops before exiting.

"Let's walk together to the shuttle," he says.

"That would be great, but I want to get a printout of my study on Charlie so I can show Mom."

"She'll love that. I bet she'll frame it." That statement brings on emotion that I must stuff.

"Yeah, she probably will."

"Want me to come with you?"

"No, Al's going to join me and I kind of want a moment alone with him. I'll meet you on the shuttle."

My dad clears his throat uncomfortably as Al approaches. "Okay, sweetie." He hugs me before leaving. I spot Colsam standing just outside the door to escort everyone to the shuttle.

"I'm going to join you?" Al asks.

"Yes, in a toast of celebration of our freedom," I say as soon as my dad's out of earshot. Then, I hand Al a chocolate milk and hold one for myself. We clink or rather thud them together and then gulp the liquid down.

Like father, like daughter. Thanks, Dad, for the information on isolating tryptophan. The milk studies have actually come in quite handy.

Once done, Al and I walk to the door together hand in hand. Part way there he begins to slump into me. As we get to the door, I wave to Colsam. He approaches and I move Al's hand over his shoulders. I kiss Al on the cheek and then begin talking with Colsam.

"It's been a long time since I've walked to a shuttle," Colsam says. "I was able to get Viscerous and Albina onboard."

When I see Al's head fall onto Colsam's shoulder, I pat Colsam's back, and head back inside.

Once they're gone, I begin walking down the hallway I've never been in. This is where Cromwell instructed me to go. When I reach the second door, I pause and put my forehead against the wall. I look both ways, wondering if I could sprint to an escape without risking those I care for. I wasn't able to work with them to organize the rebellion in time.

Before I'm able to run, I see Cromwell walking down the hall. I straighten myself up and try to look as confident as I can.

"Ah, Vienna. We finally meet for the procedure."

"Uh, yeah. So we do."

He opens the door to the room, and I see every piece of medical lab equipment available. He even has the newest technology. I see temporary organ substitute bots, healing adaptation injections, protoplasm suture machines, bio replacement bots, and more. I also see devices of torture. This is where they keep those jailed awaiting sentence. No wonder Cromwell doesn't have his quarters near here. Who could sleep with the screams of slaughter going on? Although, if anyone could, it would be him.

20

GONE

Vienna

I can't tell how many times I've hated Dr. Cromwell since my arrival on Planet Vortex. Possibly hate's too tame a word. I loathe and despise him. He's an abomination—he repels me.

"Sierra, I can call you by your given name now, can't I?" He's trying to comfort me, but in my final moments, comfort's the last thing I feel.

"I guess, Dr. Cromwell. Wait, you know my real name?"

"I just want to say thank you for giving me the opportunity to save my only child. Of course, I know your real name. I also found the history on your lab computer and discovered how you figured out the anti-rejection bots."

He rolls a large cryogenic freezer bed into the room. He knows too much!

"Okay."

"In gratitude, I will give you locals so that you don't feel the pain. I know where you get your aversion to anesthesia."

"Thank you! Wait, what?"

"It was genetically passed down, of course. I'll even give you morphine if you desire."

"Can I make that decision whenever I feel fit?" He really knows! I thought at this point I'd either be void of emotion or just freaked. It turns out that I had been unable to fully conceive what I'm feeling now. I cannot believe he knows. If only I had Yesha's abort mission from the koala syringes, and it could work now.

"Sure, I'll set up an I.V. drip with a button that you can man at your own will."

Great, in my final moments before completely becoming subservient to him, the most impressive thing he can offer back is a local, morphine, and calling me by my first name.

He rolls a second bed up. The contents are enclosed within a container, but this one does not seem to require the cryogenic freeze.

"I also want to let you know that I plan on implanting your conscience and memory into a non-bio body," Cromwell says. "My plans have not gone as smoothly as I had hoped, but I was able to find you a decent non-bio."

"What do you mean your plans haven't gone the way you hoped? Aren't I here willingly giving myself for your child?"

"Well, yes, but you see, I had hoped you'd find your Dad's letter long ago. Only recently was I able to adjust the flights to Vortex from annually to monthly. Plus, it's been a bit of a task to get my families' bodies onsite. You don't really need to know about all that though."

This information is like a splinter that festered in my skin, causing infection. The only reason I've had the time to become close with everyone and why he didn't just hold me in a cell upon my arrival was all because he needed time. Here I'd thought that I'd held power over him all along. Another thing hits me. He's known the whole time! I feel like the cartoon character realizing they're suspended in the air right before they fall. Did he orchestrate my dad's note making its way to Earth? I cannot believe he's known all along. Was this some kind of sick and twisted revenge against my dad? And I didn't think Cromwell could out do his level of evil status. I was wrong.

Is that the non-bio on the second bed? "Will my non-bio body have the robotic bloodstream inhibitors for adaptation?"

"Of course. I'll also be incorporating healing adaptation."

Just like the cartoon character, I want to move my legs in a running gesture as if I can save myself from the fall.

He shrugs his shoulders.

Then he removes his son's body from the cryogenic freezer. I can see dust particles rise from the corpse of the undead body as if sunlight were beaming through, but no ultraviolet rays reach here. Dr. Cromwell then removes part of his son's brain, placing the parts in a smaller cryogenic freezer as he continues. I know my time's very limited now. Not weeks or days, but minutes.

This is not how I envisioned my last moments. Cromwell was successful in negotiating the job for me as a host body, and now, he's holding a scalpel against the back of my head and saying, the first step to relocating the memory and conscience is removing a major portion of the brain.

As the digital protoplasm blade of the scalpel cuts into my skin, Cromwell says, "You're not going to die, you'll just have a new body."

With my skin, I can feel the scalpel's entry point. Sharp pain sears in the area of my meninges even though the local should stop this. Cromwell inserts bio replacement and temporary organ substitute bots so that the tissue can stay in its freshest form for his son. This also allows my brain to continue functioning when it otherwise should not. Maybe that's why he offered the morphine drip. He knew the local could only penetrate so far.

After the scalpel, there will be an automated, robotic drill to break through my skull as he won't have the room for error as much as the bone marrow biopsy. The thought of hearing my bone crush again sends my emotions through a grinder. Both the scalpel and the drill, will navigate all the way to the cerebral cortex, eradicating the hippocampus and medial temporal lobe along the way. Oozing my brain parts out like a vacuum sucking up dust while bots move into the space. I don't think there's a name for the emotion I'm feeling right now.

You make the wrong cut, or a drill goes too deep, and the brain matter becomes useless. This is why bots and tech are used over processes by hand in these kind of maneuvers.

"You're going to be the first live subject to receive four foreign brain components," Cromwell says. "You're going to make scientific history."

I feel the path of the scalpel and bots in the back of my head and say, "That would be true, Cromwell, if this procedure wasn't illegal."

"The legal system has cost many lives with its restrictions. We are an advanced society and I refuse to allow politicians to limit my work."

So Cromwell and I remain in the medical facility with a scalpel piercing my head, and we both hear a commotion on the holograph screen, a view of outside, but the holograph video doesn't display anything other than what we expect. I'm on my side on the gurney.

The video depicts a sunny day, of course, viewing from the hidden cameras around this place. This is one of the warmest habitable planets because it is carbon mild, but a shiver runs through me on the medical table. It's so quiet here except for the chatter from those on the screen. With all of the recent conversations I've had with everyone here, the feeling I get is that I'm at my own funeral watching the visitation; I do the only thing I have left.

Lie on the table.

Breathe as evenly as I can and meditate.

I don't believe Cromwell will transplant my being into a non-bio body as he's promised. I have about five minutes left before I'll die.

After the drill has removed a two-inch by one-inch chunk of my skull, I watch the screen to be sure they have safely boarded the shuttle. That no hot spot has fried any of them. The door to the shuttle closes with a vertical slide and then disappears into the body of the ship—closure. The absence of their chatter makes the electric buzz and bone-crushing ten times louder. Then instead of the saturation of the shuttle door, I hear the suctioning of my head. Intermittent disruptions are caused by pieces of me that will never return. Why can't my body just react normally to anesthesia? This is worse than torture. No one should have to live through this. I want to scream to release this tension, but I can't. My hands and lips shake with the overload of adrenaline from the pain.

Somewhere in the astronomical units between Planet Vortex and Planet Earth are all of the people I care about. Running from this soul-crushing place.

I see Al on the screen. I thought he'd been on board asleep. What is he doing?

I'm only going through this hell so they can be safe. That was the trade I'd made.

Why didn't he go with them? He better board the emergency pod.

I look to see if Cromwell notices Al.

Cromwell's eyes are focused on the task at hand, methodically moving his gloved hands in a calculated manner. Even though I am unable to see what he's doing now, I can tell he has come to the hippocampus. This is deeper than the cerebrum; penetrating into my head like a migraine. I saw him do this with his brainchild before me. I see Al closing in on the facility instead of the emergency pod and my heart drops to my stomach. No, turn back! My eyes dart to the cryogenic freezer holding the child's brain. The tugging and pulling jumble my attention.

This procedure is not in any medical book. With the protoplasm suture machine and substitute stem cells holding the place of removed parts, I'm temporarily able to continue normal thought patterns.

Four minutes.

The suction moves higher in my head; different matter is jiggly like Jell-O. Never thought I'd see that. I'm going to be sick. This is awful.

Cromwell and I are on the brink of scientific discovery, the suction blazing a trail through my brain, I decide to look at the brainchild's body for the rest of the procedure.

I know that if I look at the screen to try to see Al again, I'll draw Cromwell's attention to him and put him in danger. Though in my last living moments, I yearn to see Al's green northern light eyes one more time. Oh, Al.

Three minutes.

Then the blood runs down my face and over my eyes. I have to blink to keep it out. My last memory in this body or at all will be in about three minutes. By then all memory will be removed.

My limbic system will no longer be able to send synapses from the left to the right. My organs will begin to fail, and Cromwell will have seconds to transplant the parts that play a key role in functionality. I click the morphine because my entire being wants to freak out right now.

The four-part re-infiltration series. The cerebral cortex will be fitted into place with nerve ending sutures made at a brain surgeon's new technologically savvy pace. An inch below, the process will be repeated for the medial temporal lobe, with additional vein and artery connections due to its sheer size. Then the hippocampus will be inserted directly behind the ear. More suctioning will be needed, but this time to keep blood from blocking the surgeon's view. The last shot, the cerebellum, will then be fitted into place. As skull and skin are replaced and stapled, Cromwell will have the first cognizant conversation with his child in years.

"Sorna would be so happy to have our child back," Cromwell says.

I only have minutes left. And, I won't be able to warn Al. My muscles tense.

"Be still."

Two minutes.

I continue to feel the pushing and prodding, and think, *Cromwell, you want your child back, here you go. Until Al catches up to you and kills you both.* My thoughts are very confused right now. Is that hope logical? Yes, Al's one tough man. So is Cromwell. Hope. Fear.

One minute.

Mom, Dad, I love you! Al you are my first, my one and only true love.

Before I completely black out to the unknown afterlife, I see the wall between this room and the next lower. What I see then brings so much pain, it's as if the flame-throwing guard put his club down my throat and engulfed my insides in flames. My mom lies on a gurney. Sorna's body on the gurney next to her as well as another non-bio container. I sincerely hope Cromwell's not lying. My mom looks as if the life has already been drained out of her. Her eyes are closed, but then they open and look directly at me. She doesn't speak, but I hear her.

Sierra, everything's going to be okay.

But, I was trying to save those I love. What are you doing here? I don't open my mouth to speak. Then it hits me. I guess her studies on telepathy have come further than I realized, but how am I communicating with her the same way?

We don't have time to explain everything now. I was on board the unscheduled shuttle. Thank goodness we share the talent in telepathy. I'll see you on the other side.

The blackout hits before I can communicate more.

21
TIME LEAP

Al

SHORTLY AFTER RETURNING FROM THE STEM CELL harvesting center, I pull Sierra aside. "I know what Cromwell has planned for you."

"What? But, how?"

"I snuck into the desk in his office."

"Al, you know we heard you in the tunnels. You have to be careful."

"I'm fine, Sierra. He's going to do something to you that's never been done before."

"I know."

"What? And you're just going to let it happen?"

"It's the only way to get people off this planet and end procedures here safely."

"No, I've found a way you can do that and still be safe."

"Really, how?"

I explain to her how we can clone her so that she won't have to do what she's willing to do. Because she's not injured with a vulture beak plunge or dying of a fatal disease, a clone will work. Storage of the clone may still prove difficult but not impossible. For the first time I witness her break, really break. She's been so strong and beautiful through everything, but I don't think she ever believed that someone would actually be willing to save her. I don't think it even crossed her mind. Maybe she's more damaged than me.

"Can we alter my clone to have assassin skills? It would serve Cromwell right."

"I think we can do that. What, it's okay for your clone but not for Yesha?"

She fake punches me in the arm.

It takes some time to organize everything. Not only is the cloning process new to us but strategizing the switch and how to hide her away but also get her on the shuttle proves to be a real pain especially keeping up pretenses, so Cromwell doesn't suspect anything. Sierra built a ladder over the wall that we end up using. Through it all, we never planned for possible side effects. We didn't even conceive the notion to think of them. Sierra has phantom feelings similar to a lost limb. I remember those. Sierra feels what her clone feels. I never hypothesized that.

———

"You need to practice meditation with the clone. It will go over easier with you. She can't see me if we want her to act like I would act."

"Are you sure? I've never really been into the whole meditation thing."

"It's simple. Just give it a try, please."

"Okay."

"Okay, this is what you'll show her. Sit in a butterfly position."

"Are you kidding me?"

"No, now breathe in."

I follow her direction but secretly glance at her when she's not looking.

"Good, now imagine a large circle."

———

"When she gives the go ahead for the shuttle and procedures ending, that's your cue to set everything in place for the first attack," I tell Colsam.

"She's okay with that?"

"Yes and No."

"Damn it, Al."

We're back in our secret meeting place.

"I know, I know."

"Well, not only has Theopat recruited more but exoneration is definitely within reach now."

"Good. It's about time we bring an end to this place."

"When you're right, you're right."

———

"I can feel her. She thinks she's me. It's so surreal," Sierra says aloud to the group and I'm taken aback. I'm only able to watch them on our secret shuttle camera as I exited to be sure everyone boards the emergency pod. Every part of my being wants to be there with her and hold her in my arms.

She's on the shuttle and all should be well but Sierra's mind is wrapped up with everything her clone's seeing.

Septimus as well as everyone else looks very concerned.

"It's Mom. We can't leave!"

Sierra's becoming hysterical and Septimus is following close behind. Luckily, Colsam gave Viscerous some of the "sleeping pill" milk that Sierra's clone attempted to give me. It's crazy how her clone has acted just as Sierra would have had we never figured out the clone idea. She's just picking up right where Sierra would have.

Viscerous hands them both a cup. "Calm down, you two. We won't be able to help your mom if you're not thinking straight."

I'm so glad Viscerous is with them. All jokes aside, he's one of the purest men I know. As soon as they're drifting off and I've radioed Viscerous to let him know the plan so he can keep everyone on the shuttle calm, I exit the emergency pod to join Colsam in the revolution and save Sierra's mom. I knew Cromwell wasn't being honest with her. He always has a trick up his sleeve. He didn't even include Sierra's mom in his secret file.

———

The heat of a flame-throwing club brushes my cheek as I shove Colsam aside to keep him from being burned.

"The neutralizer shut off. We better get that thing back on," Colsam yells above the fighting matches.

"What do you think I'm doing?" I run as fast as I can trying to not look at the injured.

As soon as I flip the switch and the neutralizer is back up and running hand to hand combat resumes. I return to the task of confiscating all weapons.

When I've locked the last one away, a shift seems to occur in the crowd. I catch banter between two locked in a hold.

Then, I spot another pair laughing and slapping each other on the back.

"What are we even fighting for?" I hear someone say.

It's only a matter of time before we have full control of the facility. The World Government officials that Theopat recruited should arrive just in time.

A shuttle takes off. It's not the emergency pod, thank goodness. But, that means it must be Cromwell's. What, does he have a whole military aviation unit of shuttles here unbeknownst to anyone else? I point to the shuttle and shake Colsam's shoulder.

"Guess we're not going to be able to have him arrested today," he says.

"Nope. I'm more worried about Sierra's mom."

We run to Viscerous' old holding cell. My heart's pounding in my chest. I was too busy with the revolt to get here in time. The cell's empty apart from gurneys and medical equipment. I have failed! I've let her down. She'll never believe anyone's really going to help her again. I'm the one who damaged her this time. She only came here to free her dad and now her mom's gone. Of all the things I know, I know the loss of a parent is worse. How can I make it up to her? Can we rescue her mom? Could we find her brother and get them all back together?

22
FINALE

Vienna

Seeing Earth again is amazing. We'd been unable to negotiate a landing for the shuttle, as the timing isn't protocol, so we're being forced to make a near-space sky-dive. The process first took place a hundred and a half or so years ago.

Looking at the Earth from our pod, I don't see how this can be possible.

Viscerous and Albina volunteer to go first. They're excited about the prospect, crazy fools.

When Albina makes the first jump, it looks like a suicide mission. She becomes a white dot and then disappears out of sight within seconds. Viscerous does the same but we can hear that all is going wellwe'll so Dad, Theopat, and I follow suit. In her excitement to see Earth, Theopat asks to go after Viscerous and Albina and neither my dad nor I argue.

"I love you. See you on land," my dad says before jumping.

"Love you too."

It's hard to wait the allotted time as I can hear dad's breathing intensify.

I jump and it's wicked fast. We're over 600 miles per hour and it's nuts, flipping like crazy. I'm scared the parachute won't engage in time but the loud announcement from ground control ensures that won't happen.

Once I land I try to hug the Earth. I'm so happy to be here.

———

Being back in the apartment after everything we've been through is surreal. Having Dad here again is beyond compare. Right now he's walking around looking at all of the multidimensional prism photos. I notice that Mom somehow rescued all of the ones with him and put them back in place.

"It's been so long since I've seen these. I wish we could go back to that time," Dad says.

"I suggest adding eggplant for a complete meal," I hear Kitchen say.

"No, thank you. Hey, why does Kitchen keep suggesting gross things for me to add?" Viscerous yells down the hall.

"Yeah, go, run!" Albina yells at a voltball game she's watching via projected visual and sound transmissions.

The apartment has never felt this alive and yet something's missing.

Then I hear a squeal from my bedroom and walk to check it out.

"Look at all this couvrir! Closet is amazing. We need to add to the inventory." Theopat exclaims.

While my apartment's bustling, the rest of us have been separated after finally coming together. I figured out that it would be better to work as a team instead of trying to go it alone against Cromwell but that's not even an option now. I'm on Earth with my dad at last—but Mom's not here. It is nice having Viscerous and Albina stay with us though. It's also been a blast taking Theopat to all the tourist attractions. I've decided to go by Vienna to not confuse my clone…who still doesn't know she's a clone. She hasn't woken from Cromwell's vial procedure.

Al, Colsam, and Yesha are on Vortex dealing with the revolution aftermath. While we're on different planets, the World Government has now attached all Counter Friction strings. They somehow got word of the revolution and decided it was high time. They developed new processes to get around the limited bandwidth. This will be good for us because we can communicate even though we're apart.

Because I'm not going it alone ever again if I can help it.

———

Coming Soon from Fire & Ice Young Adult Books
Transformed Nexus #2
OMITTED PIECES

———

Don't miss your next favorite book!

Join the Fire & Ice mailing list
www.fireandiceya.com/mail.html

OMITTED PIECES

TRANSFORMED NEXUS #2

Chapter One
Planet Scepter

Sierra's Clone

I AWAKE HUNGRY AND THIRSTY. IS THIS WHAT THE afterlife is? I never expected Dr. Cromwell to follow through on his promise to put my conscience and memory in a qualified body. I feel the hunger again and rise to find myself in a tropical forest. I'm surrounded by a lush green, but the color is unlike any I've seen before. It's almost as if the leaves are neon shining off of their surroundings. My body knows what to look for even though I don't.

Where am I? What planet have I been transported to? Where's Mom? I look down at it, this hourglass figure. I'd never been blessed with such curves in my sixteen-year-old body. I wonder if my dad will recognize me in this new one. I wonder if Al will still love me after everything. I also try to map out how to get home, but it's all too much for this newfound body and I quickly find myself napping under a sea of green.

I'm awakened by a series of clicks.

"Vex, how'd you get here?"

"I told you your mission was full of danger."

"How long has it been since I lost consciousness?"

"I calculate two weeks and five days since the new you left Planet Vortex."

"Where's Al? Did the shuttle make it to Earth?"

There's a stream of clicks and beeping. "My universe data scan shows the Al you are asking about still has a pulse. You are talking about the Al you met on Planet Vortex, right."

My heart warms, it beams. "Yes. Wait, your universe data scan, what's that?"

"The World Government equipped all clopils with new scanners and applied all Counter Friction strings when the Planet Vortex revolution hit the news. I also show that everyone who had been on your scheduled shuttle made it to Earth. The processes at the medical facility ended too but more on that later. We need to locate your mother."

Mom, are you okay? I try to reach her.

I'm fine. Just need to figure out where I am exactly.

"Sierra, there's much at stake. We must embark on our journey at once," Vex says.

Ommited Pieces will be available Spring 2021

THANK YOU FOR READING

Did you enjoy this book?

We invite you to leave a review at the website of your choice, such as Goodreads, Amazon, Barnes & Noble, etc.

DID YOU KNOW THAT LEAVING A REVIEW…

- Helps other readers find books they may enjoy.
- Gives you a chance to let your voice be heard.
- Gives authors recognition for their hard work.
- Doesn't have to be long. A sentence or two about why you liked the book will do.

ABOUT THE AUTHOR

Stephanie Hansen is a PenCraft Award winning author. Her short story, *Break Time*, and poetry has been featured in Mind's Eye literary magazine. The Kansas Writers Association published her short story, *Existing Forces*, appointing her as a noted author. She has held a deep passion for writing since early childhood, but a brush with death caused her to allow it to grow. She's part of an SCBWI critique group in Lawrence, KS and two local book clubs. She attends many writers' conferences including the New York Pitch, Penned Con, New Letters, All Write Now, Show Me Writers Master Class, BEA, and Nebraska Writers Guild conference as well as Book Fairs and Comic-Cons. She's a member of the deaf and hard of hearing community.

www.authorstephaniehansen.com
www.authorstephaniehansen.com/blog

facebook.com/writer.stephaniehansen

twitter.com/hansenwriter

instagram.com/stephaniehansenauthor

pinterest.com/writershansen

goodreads.com/writerstephaniehansen

Made in the USA
Columbia, SC
18 August 2023

21828205R00145